William Kirkus

Only to be Married

A novel

William Kirkus

Only to be Married
A novel

ISBN/EAN: 9783337052515

Printed in Europe, USA, Canada, Australia, Japan

Cover: Foto ©Andreas Hilbeck / pixelio.de

More available books at **www.hansebooks.com**

ONLY TO BE MARRIED.

A Novel.

BY

Mrs. FLORENCE WILLIAMSON,

AUTHOR OF "FREDERICK RIVERS."

IN THREE VOLUMES.

VOL. I.

LONDON:

TINSLEY BROTHERS, 18, CATHERINE ST,. STRAND.

1867.

CONTENTS.

ONLY TO BE MARRIED.

CHAPTER I.

LEIGH.

"The Lord's gone out of His ordinary way to bless me to-day; my wife's confined o' twins."

Such was the announcement of the advent into the world of Martha Wilson and her brother John, with which their father astonished his three most intimate friends on the morning of the first of April, 1830. Martha was never superstitious, but she could not forgive a mysterious Providence for sending her into the world on that particular day. It seemed as if she were doomed to be an " April

fool " as long as she lived, and had been
written down an ass in the first line of her
biography. All through life she fancied that
there was in her character, or, at least, in her
destiny, a something crooked that could not be
made straight; as if she were fated to be for
ever either jest or jester. But at any rate, it
was on April fool's day that she was born, and
she couldn't alter it.

As to John, he died about five hours after
his birth; parted from all the more easily after
so short an acquaintance. Even five days
would have made it wonderfully harder for the
eccentric old father and gentle feeble mother
to put him into his little coffin, and bury him
out of their sight. Martha was as plump a
baby as baby could be; and, considering how
easily she exhausted the maternal resources, it
seemed a good thing that her tiny twin brother
had gone to be taken better care of elsewhere,
and had left her alone. There never was such

a baby, excepting the last of your own, good reader, if you have any; and Mrs. Wilson's nurse was perfectly certain that the little stranger had smiled at her before she was a whole day old.

The friends to whom, in the words I have quoted above, Mr. Wilson announced the singular mercy of the Lord, were three maiden ladies. They were by no means common old maids. They had no simpering affectations or fascinating sentimentalisms. They were hard-working women of business; managing a shop of their own in the busiest thoroughfare in Manchester, with an energy and success that many a *man* of business regarded with envy and surprise. A fourth sister, an old maid also, kept house for them in one of the healthiest and pleasantest of Manchester suburbs. They built the house themselves; or rather, as it is necessary to be exact in speaking of such self-helping maidens, they had it built for them. A capital detached house it was, with trusty foundations and solid walls; built for living in, and not for immediate sale. It was a perfect model of ventilation and good draining, and every nook and corner was furnished with some cupboard or closet, so that even those four tidiest of maiden ladies could never lack a place for everything. Almost the most difficult task they ever had was to find a name for the new house. There was no end of friendly suggestions offered for their assistance. Mr. Wilson suggested "Ebenezer Cottage," as combining humility with gratitude. "Rose Cottage," "Paradise Place," "Home of Peace," "The Four Sisters," with scores more of ridiculous names, were proposed by their various friends. But none of these would suit. In fact, they had almost made up their minds to leave the naming of their new abode to the genius of the postman; when, in a moment of inspiration, the fourth sister, who was christened Betsey, solved the problem with which they had so long been struggling.

"We shall never get a name for our house," said Mary, the eldest.

"Why not ask the postman the address of Miss Rhodes," said Sarah, the second, "and see what he says it is; for of course he's sure to know."

"Nonsense, Sally," said Jane, "he can't know our address till we've got one."

"And we've got one," said Betsey. "Polly just gave it to us; it's 'Our House.' What could be better?"

So it was settled at last. "The Misses Rhodes, Our House, Cheetham Hill, Manchester." And a very snug house it was. But it was at the shop that Mr. Wilson had called to communicate the news of his unexpected and undeserved honour. Not being the least affected, and knowing quite well, as a fact in natural history, that there are such things as twins, Sarah and Betsey and Jane congratulated their old friend on his new treasures.

"Ah!" said the old gentleman, "it's the Lord's doing."

"And it's marvellous in our eyes," said Betsey.

"Ah," said the old gentleman again, with a strange mixture of parental affection and Calvinistic complacency, "Jacob have I loved, and Esau have I hated. Will they both be Jacobs, Miss Sarah?"

"I don't think it's at all likely," said mischievous Betsey, "for you've just told us one was a girl."

He could not quite help laughing, though he thought Betsey was approaching too nearly to the jesting which is not convenient. But he wished them a cheerful good-morning, and went to his shop, a few doors from the Rhodeses. Somehow he couldn't work. He

grew restless and melancholy ; he kept thinking of his wife, and wondering, with a strange
foreboding that he could not master, whether
all was still well at home. At last he could
resist the impulse no longer ; he left business,
never too busy with him, to the charge of his
foreman, and returned to his house. They had
just laid little Johnnie in the cradle, dead.

So, as I said before, Martha was to have no
rival or partner to rob her of any share of the
parental fondness ; and perhaps too, the little
brother, sleeping so quietly in the white cradle,
had left her his cares and troubles also. But at
any rate, they did not burden her yet ; and her
sleep seemed not less peaceful than his, as she
lay by her mother's side. The poor mother was
speechlessly weeping. It seemed so hard that
she should be robbed of the joy after all her
pain ; and they had three girls already. Would
it not have been better if little Martha had
been taken, and the only boy left ? And then

she pressed the little sleeper closer to her bosom, and almost felt that she had been cherishing murderous thoughts against her babe, and half feared that God might take her also, to punish the mother's rebellion.

But God did not take her. On the contrary, it seemed quite plain that he intended her to stay a very long time, for better or for worse, in this very puzzling world, where perhaps more people lose their way than find it. She had as much health as all her three sisters put together, and being positively " the last appearance " of a baby in Mr. Wilson's family she seemed to be having her benefit, " and producing an immense sensation " every day. And yet her father could never persuade himself that she could by any device be kept alive for a whole year, unless she were taken in the summer months to the sea-side ; or to some of the delicious villages, of which there are not a few within easy reach of Manchester. The other three girls were at school for the most part, and at any rate, none of them was the baby; and they had got fairly seasoned to this world, before going out of town had become the fashion in Mr. Wilson's circle. Indeed, it was hardly in fashion yet. But somehow or other he could not bear to think of any kind of harm coming to the baby—they had begun to call her Patty by this time; so, if nobody else went from home in the hot summer, Patty and her mother were sure to be seen at some watering-place, or walking together through woods and meadows, over hills and moors, in the cool quiet country. And if Patty did not need it, it was quite plain her mother did.

Besides, going to the sea-side, or especially into some quiet inland village, was not quite so much going from home in their case, as most people must often have found it. Who does not know the torturing delight of a month at the sea-side? We leave a quiet home where there is a place for everything, and where everything is generally in its place; where, if we want anything, we ring the bell and tell the servant to bring it; where, in the privacy and safety of the time-honoured Englishman's castle, we can do just what we like; and we go to a place where everything is confusion and disappointment, where half the house is inhabited by people who are total strangers to us, and who very likely complain that we are extremely disagreeable, and that they are being incessantly disturbed either by our own merriment, or the nocturnal lamentations of our children. "Well, my dear," says the wife to her husband, "you can't expect to be so comfortable in lodgings as you are at home." Just as if the father of a family had not left home for the purpose of being rather more comfortable than usual; spending three pounds a week for apartments, and a whole mint of money for travelling expenses in the hope of special enjoyment. More-

over, all the prettiest watering-places are the
fashionable watering-places ; and then, instead
of being more at your ease than you were in
No. 1, Any Street, you discover, to your horror,
that the customs of the place that you have
paid so much to visit require you to dress in
your best clothes, and show yourself off on the
parade—and, in fact, do everything that from
the bottom of your soul you most utterly de-
test doing. And at last, when all is over, with
what profound melancholy does a man tell the
tale of his summer's trip to the little circle of
his friends and acquaintances. " Charming
place," he says, " glorious parade, splendid sea,
crowds of fashionable company "——and then,
to his most intimate friend, he relieves his mind
by improper language and honesty. For after
all, the great benefit of going from home in the
summer is simply this, that one finds out what
a blessing it is that summer comes only once a
year.

But the watering-place to which Mrs. Wilson
and Patty were in the habit of going every
other summer was Blackpool. A fashionable
watering-place too, in its way; perhaps the most
fashionable in Lancashire, and much more
fashionable than beautiful. Excepting the sea,
which is what people call a fine sea, there is
really nothing worth visiting Blackpool for.
But Patty and her mother had relations who
lived there, and with whom they could really
be at home. Like the natives and regular inhabitants of the place,—the people who not
only bask in the sun in the brightest weather,
but who also get the cold salt water blown into
their faces all through the dreary winter,—they
could defy the tyranny of those fashions which
were meant only for holiday-makers, for those
unhappy mortals who have left a comfortable
home to enjoy themselves in uncomfortable
apartments. But Blackpool was not the place
they liked best to go to ; it was far pleasanter

to spend the summer months at Leigh. Every other year, in that most delicious hamlet, they spent four or five weeks with old Joseph Platt, who was an uncle of the maiden Rhodeses. In fact, before they went to Manchester he had been as good as a father to them, not to say, better. For their father had done them the gross injustice of being perseveringly poor ; and dying, when Betsey was only five years old, had left a blessing and four girls to his wife's brother, old Joseph Platt, aforesaid.

Mrs. Rhodes had died a year before her husband ; and though very few human beings die of anything like a broken heart, yet poor Mrs. Rhodes's death did really kill her husband. He was a man with not half spirit enough to bear his infirmity, whatever his infirmity might be—a most amiable man, who was never allowed to go out alone with more than a shilling in his pocket, because he couldn't resist the temptation of giving all his loose money to the first beggar-woman with a baby, who was clever enough to invent a pitiful autobiography and burst into tears. He might have been a rich man if he had been a little harder, or even without being really hard at all ; but he was very anxious to be just, and very ready to be kind, and the people with whom he had to do took every sort of mean advantage of him, doing their wicked best to reverse the benediction, " Blessed are the meek, for they shall inherit the earth." He never quite understood how badly he was treated ; in fact, it would have given him far more pain to know that his neighbours were so ungenerous, than even his own want of success caused him. But, at any rate, he knew quite well that he was not successful, and many a time he had lain awake all night thinking how disappointed his wife must be, and wondering what he would do with the girls. And when his wife had left him, he used to fancy in his loneliness, that perhaps she had died of some secret hidden trouble that she had been too brave-hearted to tell him of; and, at any rate, he had nobody left to talk with, and he did not the least know what to do in all the bewilderment of his ever-increasing ill-success. There was nobody any longer to take all his money out of his pocket, except a shilling; nobody to manage the servants and look after the children. He never could find anything he wanted in his own wardrobe; and when plates and dishes were broken, and silver spoons and forks were lost, and the dinners were badly cooked, and all was muddle and confusion together, he never could sufficiently brace himself to give anybody a good scolding, however much it might have been deserved, and reduce his chaos into some sort of order. So, in fact, he gave it up; gave everything up; gave up in fine—the ghost.

About then the Rhodeses went to live with their uncle, old Joseph Platt, who gave them a

much better education than rustic Leigh was
in the habit of thinking necessary, though it included no showy accomplishments. What was
the use, for instance, of learning French, German,
or Italian, when no living inhabitant of Leigh
could remember ever having seen a foreigner?
Dancing, again, was sinful, not to mention that
there were no young men to dance with in Mr.
Platt's circle of friends. As to music, there
was only one house in Leigh in which a piano
was to be found, and that was the house of
old Aaron Higginbotham, the solicitor; a very
good solicitor too, and one who would also have
been a good husband and a good father, but for
an inveterate habit of drinking. His horse
knew every public-house between Leigh and
Manchester, and never failed to stop at every
one of them, whoever happened to be driving
him. Many a time had the safety of the man
depended on the sagacity of the beast; and
when he reached home rather more drunk than

usual, it was quite uncertain whether he would
call his daughters to family prayers, or turn
them out into the garden and bolt the doors.
But, in spite of his intemperance, he managed
the affairs of his clients with great discretion;
and when, after a long sickness brought about
by his habitual intemperance, he was well
enough to take his place in the large square
pew at Leigh church, he never failed to request
the clergyman to read publicly before the
thanksgiving, " Aaron Higginbotham desires to
return thanks to Almighty God for recovery
from a dangerous illness." Very merry girls
his daughters were, in spite of the discomforts
that often resulted from their father's infirmity,
and they played, and sang, and danced far better
than could have been expected from country
lasses. But old Mr. Platt did not like it; he
thought singing songs, and dancing, and poor
old Higginbotham's drunkenness, were somehow
all of a piece, and that it was better to be on

the safe side.   So the only music the Rhodeses
learned was the psalm and hymn tunes required
for public worship in the Methodist chapel in
Leigh.   They went once a week to the prac-
tising, where there was a fiddle and a flute, and
a bass-viol, and a leader, whose furious energy
and stentorian voice were, perhaps, sufficient
compensation for want of skill and taste.   Then,
as they grew up, they became more and more
useful on old Joseph Platt's farm, and could
milk, and make butter and cheese, and brew as
well as anybody.   But they had a kind of
ambition, and, at any rate, a very proper inde-
pendence of spirit, and they did not choose to
be a burden on their good-natured uncle ; so
he very generously set them up in business in
a quiet way in Manchester, where more and
more they prospered as all good people will,
who have really made up their minds what to
do, and who stick to the doing of it.

Mr. Platt was very old, nearly ninety, when

Mrs. Wilson and Patty used to visit him ; but
he was a very cheerful old man, knowing and
known by almost everybody in Leigh and its
neighbourhood. There was no end to his
merry stories, and there was no young child
with whom Patty felt half so much at home as
she did with old Grandfather Platt. In Manchester, and even at Blackpool, she was not
allowed to go out alone, for there were many
dangerous crossings and crowded streets in
which she might get bewildered and lost. But
at Leigh she could wander for hours in Mr.
Platt's own fields, and she might have lain
down and slept on the king's highway without
the slightest danger of being run over. So she
would often be away from the farm, excepting
at meal times, almost all the day long, walking
till she was tired, and then sitting down to rest
on the grass, or on a stile, or on some great
stone by the river's side. Her favourite walk
was down through the fields to the river, and

then along the water side till it was time to go
home again, and somehow or other she was
always punctual, though her only clock was the
sun and the shadows.

And so Mrs. Wilson and old Mr. Platt were all
the more frightened when one evening Patty
did not come back at all. She was then nearly
fourteen years old, and it was late indeed
before they began to feel seriously uneasy.
Patty, they felt sure, knew her way in all
directions for miles round old Mr. Platt's farm,
and she was a strange child, finding company when almost every other girl of her own
age would have been terrified by intolerable
loneliness. She had scarcely any companions,
even in Manchester; none of those bosom
friends that are so abundant in early childhood,
and so few in those riper years when we so
much more deeply need them. At Leigh her
choicest friends seemed to be the calves, and
lambs, and pigeons, and the little fishes playing

in the river—a river so clear and bright that
you could see almost every grain of sand at
the bottom of it—and the wild flowers and
mosses in the wood that lay between the Leigh
Road at the top of a high hill and the river at
the bottom. She had left the farm as soon as
dinner was over ; that is to say, between one
and two o'clock, and walked quietly across the
fields to the river side. She sat there for perhaps an hour on a great smooth stone that had
come to be her favourite seat, watching the fishes,
and then watching a pair of blackbirds whose
nest was at the other side, trying to count how
many times they carried home food to their
little ones; and then she thought she would go
across the bridge, and along the lane at the
other side, to see an old woman, a tenant of
old Mr. Platt's, and who had gained her confidence by telling wild stories of the old times
of Leigh history, which were now almost fading
away from the memory of men. The old

woman persuaded her to stay with her till tea-time, and she was only too glad to linger and hear the end of a story that had been begun a week before. It was still light when she left the old woman's house, for it was considerably above the level of the river, and although the sun had already sunk below the hill on the other side and there was no moonlight, it seemed as if in these long Midsummer days not even the nights could be dark. So Patty set off about half past seven o'clock to return to the farm, no way hurrying, and intending to ramble through the wood to the Leigh Road, instead of taking her ordinary way through the meadows. So she went along over the bridge, over the stile, into the wood, up the steep winding pathway, until she grew quite tired, and sat down to rest, and think over the story the old woman had been telling her. She sat thinking and day-dreaming she could never tell how long, till she fairly fell asleep, for,

evening though it was, the air was hotter and
closer than it had been all the day through.
When she woke she could hardly see her own
hand ; the wood was thick, and it was " the
leafy month of June." She could see no
glimpse of sky, for indeed it was black with
clouds, and in fact, almost before she had come
to understand where she really was, there was
a bright blue flash of lightning and a loud roar
of thunder that almost paralysed her with fear.
For thunder and lightning was the one thing
in all nature that utterly terrified her. But,
frightened or not, it was no use sitting where
she was, and so, slowly and carefully moving
her hands before her, she walked downwards
and downwards along the steep winding path,
till at last she came to the well-known stile
and heard the washing of the river. How well
she knew and loved it ; and yet how black and
cold it seemed. And now her way would lie,
for some hundreds of yards at least, among

great smooth stones, among which, in fear and darkness, she might easily fall or lose her way. Indeed she did lose her way, and instead of turning towards the meadows, she turned towards the bridge. It was a very narrow bridge, about four feet wide, with no rail or wall on either side;—a bridge, from which only a few weeks before the village doctor, coming home drunk, in a dark wild night, had fallen into the river and, washed down over some twenty water-falls, had been at last taken out bruised and mangled almost past recognition. With speechless horror she found herself on the middle of this bridge; she dared not move either backward or forward ; a single false step, and she must fall into the water without the faintest hope of rescue. Wondering what she could do, bitterly and vainly regretting the delay and weariness that had brought her into so much fear and danger, she heard the firm footsteps of a man walking down the lane at the other side, and turning to cross the bridge. She tried to call to him to ask his help, to implore him at least not to harm her, but she was utterly mastered by terror, and fell down senseless.

" Poor child," said the stranger, " how cold she is! What can I possibly do with her? How strange for such a young girl to be here on such a night as this."

CHAPTER II.

THE old woman, whose story had tempted Patty to stay so long was, as I have said, one of Mr. Platt's tenants, and one of the oldest inhabitants of Leigh. Yet she was not a native of the place, and nobody seemed clearly to know who she was, or whence she had come. She had not the broad, rough dialect of the Leigh people, and she seemed to have had more schooling than Leigh manners and customs could account for.

"Where did I leave off, Patty?" said old Lucy Wylde.

"Begin it again, granny, won't you?" said Patty. "You can hurry over the first part; but I should like to hear it all at once."

"God bless you, lovey," said the old woman; "it's a hard life that makes a pretty story. Years ago, long before Clayton's factory was built and the Hall on the other side of the new bridge, there was, where the new Hall stands now, a dull old house with broken windows, almost tumbling to pieces for want of somebody to take care of it. The garden was full of weeds, and the wall and fence were broken down wherever boys or stray cattle had minded to pass through. Nobody seemed to care what was done for the old Hall, and it would have been but a dull house at the best. There was the dark wood behind, and only a footway through it to the Leigh Road; and the old bridge was narrower and more dangerous than the one just below. A house like that would have needed happy hearts and merry laughs, and true, true love to make it homelike."

"Why, granny, you look as dull," said

Patty, "as if you'd been moping there yourself all that time."

"Nay, lovey, I'm not dull," said old Lucy;
"it's all over now, but it was a weary time."

She seemed almost living the story over in
silent memory instead of telling it, so long
her pause seemed to Patty.

"Well, granny, go on. Who lived there?"

"Ay, ay, who lived there, do you say?
Well, the *old* Hall was standing, lovey, as I
told you; it was what they called in Chancery, but I don't know what that means.
Only it was all tumbling to pieces, and nobody
seemed able to give orders to have it set right.
But at last a man came down all the way from
London to look at the place. He had the wall
and fences mended and the old house made
something decent-like; and he lived there for
two or three months till all was finished to his
mind. Then he put old Betty Tyler there to
be housekeeper—poor old body, it's years now

since old Betty's gone—and told her she might have two servants to keep all in order, and then went away again to London. So old Betty did as he bid her, and Mary Briggs and Ann Ashton were the lasses she had to help her. It wasn't to call a hard place; but, for all their bits o' sweethearting and good wages, it was but dull living in the old Hall. 'We couldn't make anybody hear us,' old Betty used to say, 'if we were all getting murdered together.' And many a stormy night I sat with her there, and we've half trembled to hear the wind in the wood, and the splashing and roaring of the water, and like a shrieking and howling all round. Betty was a good old body, a Methodist, and many a night when it was thundering and lightening, and howling and yelling all round, she'd get out her little Bible and read and pray; and 'Lucy,' she'd say, 'we'll be found watching; perhaps the Lord's coming.'"

"I can't bear thunder and lightning," said Patty.

"Well, lovey," said the old woman, "it never hurt old Betty Tyler. But, however, one dark, wild night, just about the beginning of September, there came a loud knocking at the door, and startled all of us, for I was keeping Betty company a bit. We all went to the door together, and there stood the gentleman from London, and two strong men, holding between them a lady, who seemed crazed-like and stared about her without saying a word, like a poor mad thing.

"'Get her in,' said the gentleman, 'and then you go over the bridge, Tom, and fetch her luggage. Tie the horse to a post, and then the driver can help you. Betty, get a nice bright fire and lights in the parlour, and in the two best bedrooms.'

"Of course Betty did as she was told, but we'd a deal of whispering and wonderment, and were half frightened of the poor pretty darling, though she looked so pale and weak. However, she was very tired, and we soon got her to bed, and one of us was to sleep with her. 'Sleep you with her, Lucy,' they said ; 'you're knowinger-like than us, and you'll manage her best, and you can call us if there's any need.' So the clock was just striking eleven as I went up to her room. She started when she saw me and gave a sort of scream ; but I sat down by her and kissed her, and she began to cry, poor dear, and it seemed to comfort her, and I cried too, lovey, you may be sure.

" 'Has my guardian gone away ?' she said. 'Mr. Windham, has he gone ?'

" 'No, my dear,' I said, 'it's not likely he'd go and never say good-bye. He's sleeping in the large room at the back.'

" 'I wish he would never wake again !' she said, and her eyes flashed and glared. 'More cruel than all devils ! Only one day together, and he tore us apart, and swore we should never see each other more. O God! how couldst thou bear to see our helpless misery?'

"And then she wrung her hands and cried piteously, sitting on the bed and rocking herself backwards and forwards, till she grew quite faint and dead-like, and so fell asleep. But over and over again she kept starting up and calling for Edwin. 'Come, come, my own Edwin, they're taking me away. Save me, my love, my husband!' It was little sleep, lovey, I had that night, and when morning came she was too ill to get up—almost too ill to speak. Of course we sent for the doctor, but he was drunk before he got here, for he never could pass a beer-shop without drinking, and there was many a one between his house and the old Hall. So Mr. Windham just sent him home again and went to Manchester for another. The new doctor told us to keep her quiet and she would come round in a day or two; so as

soon as she seemed out of danger, Mr. Windham left us and went back to London. 'She'll
be sure to tell you all about it when she gets a
little better,' he said; 'all you have to do is
to be very kind to her, and see that nobody
visits her, and that she does not run away.
Make her as happy as you can, poor child.'

"It was nearly three months, for all the doctor
said, before she could walk; and all that time
I stayed with Betty and the lasses. They
seemed fair terrified. Never a sweetheart
would they have come to the old Hall. They
said it was never lucky; and besides that, God
bless 'em, they'd kind hearts, and they couldn't
bring sweethearts and love-making in *her* way,
poor thing. So it was dull enough, and all the
duller for her trying to make us cheerful.
About the end of June———"

"Well, granny, but what did she come for?
did she tell you all about it?"

"Yes, lovey, didn't I tell you? She was

what they call 'a ward in Chancery.' I don't
know what that is, but it was bad enough for
her, poor dear; for she was married, or thought
she was, and went away with her husband to
spend a happy honeymoon. They were down
in the other end of England, at a place they
call Torquay. It was the evening of the day
after their marriage,—just been married a day;
they had been walking over the downs, looking
at the blue, blue sea. I don't think there can
be such lovely water anywhere else, darling, for
I've seen it. I went down there for her, poor
thing, to try and hear news of her husband. I
asked for every place where she told me they'd
been together, and I'd have walked in every
one of their footsteps if I could have found
them; but it was no use. The people at the
hotel remembered all about it, but he'd gone
away, left all his luggage behind him, and they
half thought he'd drowned himself. But I
never told *her* that, lovey. 'Oh, Lucy, Lucy,'

she said, 'it was my last hope; and now I know I shall never see him again. Married for a day, for one day!"

And then Lucy stopped, and rocked herself backwards and forwards, and seemed to go back a score of years, and live the misery over again. Patty, too, was feeling very miserable and half afraid, but she was getting impatient for the end of the story.

"Go on, granny, go on; you have not told me half yet. It was evening, you know—the day after the wedding; what next?"

"Yes, lovey; but it's a long way to Torquay and back, and I've just been going there again. Well, they were walking in front of the hotel, thinking they'd just see the streets and the best of the shops before supper time, when she suddenly seized her husband's arm with both her hands, and said, 'Oh, Edwin! there's Mr. Windham; what can have brought him here?' He soon came up to them, and two other gen-

tlemen were with him. 'Well, sir!' said Mr.
Windham to her husband, 'do you call this
the conduct of a gentleman, to hurry this poor
trusting child away when you knew you could
never marry her?' He began to say they were
married already, and my poor darling was beginning to tell them all about it : 'Yes, guardian, we really are married; and I am very,
very happy. It was at St.——' but Mr.
Windham soon stopped them both, 'Nonsense!
nonsense!' he said; 'you might as well have
been married on the sofa. He *cannot* marry
you, poor child.' And then my poor pet grew
so frightened, she fainted away. And then
they took her into the hotel, and the gentlemen
explained to her husband all about it, and got
him to another hotel for that night, and she
never saw him any more.

"The next day they brought her here, as I
told you, lovey, one wild autumn night, and
she stayed at the old hall till the end of the

next June. That month, the very last day—
we could hardly be sure it wasn't the day after
—her pretty baby was born. She was very,
very ill, she said she was sure she must die. So
the clergyman came from Leigh to see her, and
to christen the baby, Edwin Marie, after father
and mother. 'It didn't matter,' she said, 'boys
often have girls' names abroad, and perhaps it's
the only thing that will ever remind him of his
mother.' But it was only too true that she
would never get better. She just lived ten
days after the baby was born, and then she
died. The clergyman and the doctor had persuaded her to make a will to prevent any mistake ; and she left everything that belonged to
her to her boy. Of course we had to do the
best we could with the poor little thing, and
when it was about a month old, Mr. Windham
came down from London with a nurse, and
fetched it away. The girls stayed about six
months longer at the old Hall, and then Mr.

Windham came down again from London, and paid them the wages that were due, and made them some very pretty presents besides, and then the old Hall was shut up. It soon began to look as it used to do,—the fences were broken down by every idle boy who wanted to steal a flower or fruit from the trees, and it was just as much in Chancery as ever it was. At last I suppose they got matters settled, and the old place was pulled down altogether and the new one built,—the one you know, Patty. So that's all my story, lovey, and a very dull story too. And now get your bonnet, and run home, or they'll begin to wonder where you are. The sun will soon be behind the hill, and it's rough, dangerous walking over the bridge and by the water-side."

So old Lucy bid Patty good-bye, and Patty went away, as we know already, to sleep in the wood, and lose herself in the darkness and storm.

And where was Patty now ? She was in Clayton Hall, and Edwin Marie was watching over her. How odd that the old woman should have been driven to tell her story on that particular night of all the year.

CHAPTER III.

WITH great difficulty, Edwin Forester had carried Patty from the narrow bridge to a cottage about three or four hundred yards off, close to the river side. The cottage belonged to Clayton's factory people, and the man who lived there had charge of the noble reservoirs, which secured ample water-power for the factory, even in the dryest seasons. The mill itself was in the midst of gardens, and its south wall was covered with fruit-trees. It was always scrupulously clean, admirably ventilated, altogether different from the close, dirty, unwholesome factories of Stockport and Manchester. Edwin knocked at the door of the cottage, scarcely knowing whether to leave his burden there, or get assistance to carry the poor child to Clayton's Hall, about a mile further on, close to the mill. He had to knock again and again, for the inmates were already in bed; the wind was loud, and the water was rushing by with more than its wonted roar and dash, and perhaps the inmates were in no hurry to open their doors to a perfect stranger on a dark, wild night. At last, however, Bob Vickers appeared, and wanted to know who the stranger was, and what he meant by knocking at honest people's doors on such a night, when they were only too thankful to be able to get a wink of sleep, what with wind and thunder and the river.

"But God bless us," said Bob, who had a kind heart enough under his surly manners, " what's amiss, master? What's matter with the lass? Her looks welly dead like."

" Why, I know no more than you, Vickers,"

said Forester; "I picked her up on the bridge. She seemed to have lost her way."

"On the bridge, master? Good Lord! It's not many as tumble down there on a dark night but find their way to the t'other side o' the mill wi' all their bones brocken! Poor little wench, who can her be? her's none o' our folk. Peggy, lass, get thee things on, and come down as fast as ye can, here's a poor wench seems welly dead like—look sharp."

Peggy Vickers, his wife, was soon down, and they took Patty in, and tried what they could to revive her. But she seemed utterly un-nerved, and was no sooner brought to con-sciousness than she fainted away again from sheer terror. Moreover, in a cottage where sickness was scarcely ever known, even the simplest restoratives were not to be expected; and Edwin soon made up his mind that she must be taken on to the Hall as gently and as quickly as possible. Had he not also looked

on her sweet face, and begun to feel the fasci-
nation of a little harmless mystery, a romantic
adventure? Who could tell what this maiden
might be whom he had rescued like a gallant
knight from danger and death? She was at
least beautiful, and in the morning she would
be able to tell him who she was, and he could
take her home. The Hall was not over cheerful at the best, and a new companion, so
strangely found, might help to make the dul-
ness of the country, to a young man of twenty,
somewhat less intolerable. So Vickers and
Edwin took her on to the Hall, more carrying
than leading her; not teasing her, and indeed
scarcely suffering her, to speak; and explaining
to her where she had been found, and that she
should be taken safely home in the morning.

Once at his own house, Edwin was soon able
to find means to restore Patty; and she was
soon well enough to understand where she had
been found, and to explain how she came there.

She was not at all frightened now, and her only
anxiety was for her mother and good old Mr.
Platt. But Forester assured her that he would
send one of his servants to them at once to
tell them that she was safe, and to promise
them that he would himself bring her home to
them early the next morning. In fact, he
despatched a servant for this purpose immediately, and resigned Patty to the care of his
housekeeper, that proper arrangements might
be made for her rest and comfort.

Clayton's Hall was very unlike the old Hall,
on the site of which it had been built. The
rooms were large and lofty, and furnished with
excellent taste, and in the most modern style.
It seemed to have been the intention of its
proprietor to remove everything that could
revive old associations, or remind its inmates
of the gloom and sorrow by which, for many
dreary years, the old Hall had been haunted.
Many trees had been cut down which used to

darken the windows, and the new house stood in the midst of a clear space which extended from the river to the foot of the hill. The garden was well stocked with such hardy plants as would thrive in that north country; and there were hothouses and conservatories for choice and more delicate flowers and fruits. The old bridge had been taken away, and a new one built; which formed part of a good road winding through the wood from the factory to the Leigh Road above. But as Patty lay awake, with only a dim candle and flickering fire-light lighting the large chamber which had been appropriated to her use, she could shut her eyes and fancy herself in the old Hall to which poor Marie had been brought that wild autumn night, and where her little boy was born. She lay awake thinking of old Lucy's story, and wondering what had become of Edwin Marie, and whether the new Hall was his, and whether he ever came to visit it.

Sometimes, as wild gusts of wind went howling by, and the rain beat against her windows, she trembled in her bed with fear, lest there should be some new tragedy in that lonely house in which she herself must play the chief sufferer's part. But at last she slept, a sound, dreamless, refreshing sleep—so sound and long, that the sun was high in heaven when she awoke, and remembered that she was in Clayton's Hall. She looked out from the windows on the river, and the meadows on the other side, and the factory reservoirs, and the glorious wood covering the hill with richest foliage of every tint and shade. It seemed a perfect paradise, into which surely no grief or wrong could ever come. And Patty was young, and morning was to her, what it ought to be for all of us, the gladdest, brightest, hopefullest part of all the day. It seemed to assure her that whatever darkness there was in the past was forgotten and forgiven, and to call her to a new life of joy and love and trust. But when we have had long years of the stern conflict of life, the morning brings us more fear than hope. It renews all our cares. It calls us to battle and danger. And there is scarcely a thanksgiving we more heartily utter than this, " Thank God another day is over ! "

Edwin had been up, almost " with the lark," and had half begun to think that his young guest would never wake. He himself had scarcely slept at all, for he was almost ridiculously excited by his romantic adventure, and a little afraid lest it might scarcely bear the disenchanting light of common day. But when Patty came down he was more excited than ever ; and for a young man of twenty, and in utter forgetfulness of his wonted self-possession, far too bashful and bewildered. Young gentlemen of that age, especially if they have come from London to illuminate the rustics of some out-of-the-way country district, are perfectly certain that they are and must be the pride and glory of all God's creation, " the roof and crown of things." But Forester could only blush and stutter, and ask irrelevant questions, and make silly obvious remarks, after the manner of all young gentlemen who so far forget themselves as to be bashful.

" We have a lovely morning, Miss ——. But, indeed, I scarcely heard your name, and I've been trying to recollect it all the morning."

Thus did Mr. Edwin Forester plunge into the profoundest depths of conversational originality.

" My name is Patty Wilson, sir," said his guest ; " and I should very much like to know *your* name, that I may thank you for your great kindness. Of course I couldn't help fainting away on the bridge, could I ?"——

Here her large blue eyes, with their bright beauty and wondrous depths of thought and

inquiry, and simple trust, doubled his confusion.

"But I never meant to give trouble to anybody, least of all to a stranger."

"My name's Forester, but you need not
thank me, Miss Patty ; you've given me a
great deal of pleasure, and no trouble at all,"
said Edwin. " I'd have taken care of anybody
I found in such a place."

Here the conversation flagged. Forester was
bashful again, and had to begin the dialogue
afresh, from the invariable starting-point.

" Wonderfully different morning from last
night, Miss Wilson. The sun very much alters
the look of places, especially in the country."

" How the leaves sparkle after the rain," said
Patty, " and how fresh and clean they all look,
and how glad the birds seem to be, to find it
fine again, with plenty of worms for their little
ones. Do you live here, Mr. Forester ?"

" Well, this is my place, but I don't often

come down," he said, "it's rather slow, and I like town much better."

" Which town ?" said Patty.

" Why, *town*, Miss Wilson—London ; but somehow or other, I always spend a month or two at the Hall. I was born here, or, at least, in the old Hall. Did you ever see it, Miss Wilson ? "

" No, sir," said Patty; " when I first visited Leigh it had just been pulled down, and the workmen were busy building this."

" It was a dull old place," said Edwin ; " I could not bear it ; besides, my poor mother died there, and half the neighbourhood thought it haunted or unlucky ; no servants would stop there, and somehow everything about the place seemed blighted."

" Are you the poor little baby, sir ?" said Patty, who had quite forgotten for the moment where she was, and was thinking of old Lucy's story.

"Well, Miss Patty," said Edwin, "I'm not much of a baby now, am I? But I was a baby once, like most other people, and I was born in the old Hall, and my poor mother died when I was only a day or two old. But what did you ever hear about me?"

"Why, that's the very story old Lucy was telling me last night, that I stayed so late to hear. I was thinking about it when I fell asleep in the wood, before the storm."

"Where does old Lucy live?" asked Forester; "who is she?"

Patty told him, and would have edified him with all she knew of his own history, but for the arrival of her mother and good old Mr. Platt. Of course poor Mrs. Wilson cried to find Patty so safe and well; but they were all very grateful to Mr. Forester, and, in fact, became a very merry, happy little breakfast party. Edwin insisted on walking home with them, when he could find no excuse for keeping them at the hall any longer ; and made them promise before he left them, that they would consider him as a neighbour, and sometimes visit the house to which they had been so strangely introduced, and make it more cheerful and homelike for a young man deprived of the society and enjoyments of life in town.

Edwin Forester was, as we know already, " the litle baby," the child of disappointed love, of parents who were married only for a day. The weary chancery-suit had almost ruined his prospects, not so much by wasting his fortune, as by flattering him with vain hopes, which prevented that self-reliance and earnest effort, which might easily have made a better fortune than he expected to inherit. It was proved, however, some ten years after his mother's death, that she really was an heiress, and what the lawyers had left of her fortune, descended by her will to her son. Innocent as

she was, there really was some flaw in her marriage, which made it absolutely null and void,
and therefore her son took her name and not his
father's. He was scarcely yet released from his
legal guardians, but it had been of course quite
impossible to conceal from him the fact that
there was something strange about his parentage; some misfortune that could scarcely be
distinguished from a disgrace. It was not
among kith and kin that he had been brought
up; or, rather, his guardians were far-off relations who knew quite well that his own birth
into the world had deprived themselves of
some small fragment of a ruined inheritance.
They had never spoken gently and humanly of
his mother, but only in a dry, legal way, just
as the chancery lawyers might have talked of
her. They never indeed disgraced her memory, or perhaps their cruel wrong might have
waked the slumbering instincts of filial affection in Edwin's heart. But they treated her

with such mere indifference, that she was a
stranger to her own child; and when he came
to understand that there was a mystery about
his birth which would always need an explanation which might often be disbelieved, he
felt almost ready to resent what seemed to
him the folly, if not the unkindness, of his
mother's error. He was quite unable to ap-
preciate her pure simplicity, her fervent love,
her bitter, vain regrets, not chiefly for herself,
but for her child.

Edwin, however, had determined in a lazy
sort of way to discover who the man was who
had persuaded his mother that she was really
married to him. He wanted the whole matter
set right, to get his father to own him, if it
were worth while, to have his name changed,
if it were necessary, and somehow or other to
undo the past. Such a work is difficult enough
for everybody, but even a far easier work would
soon have exhausted the energy of a man like

Edwin Forester. Every now and then he fancied he had discovered some clue to his great mystery; somebody was somewhere or other who could tell him something. Once or twice he had been on this fruitless errand to some of the chief towns and cities on the continent, but he was always baffled in the very beginnings of his inquiries. The people to whom he had been directed knew absolutely nothing about him; and every time he tried the experiment it seemed more and more ridiculous to rehearse the secrets of his own history to some gaping stranger, who had nothing to tell him in return. So he had come at last to feel, that whenever some fresh clue was offered to him, it was his bounden duty to avail himself of it, while at the same time it was absolutely certain that all his efforts would be wasted. So in truth, every new hearsay on what had once been his great subject, degenerated into an excuse for a holiday, a country or continental tour.

It was, however, with a sharpened curiosity
that he had heard what Patty told him about
old Lucy's story. He determined to find her
out, and he began to hope, that now at last the
great secret would be discovered, and the mystery of his life solved.

Poor old Lucy had long been silent about
that sad history which was the one great fact
of her life. The servants who had been at the
old Hall when Marie was brought there, had
died or left the neighbourhood; and there was
no one in the new generation to whom old Lucy
cared to tell the story, which never faded from
her own memory, which was never absent even
from her thoughts. But somehow it was a very
heavy burden for an old woman to carry about
with her year after year; she wanted only to
find some heart that could receive and faith-
fully keep it, with enough of simple love truly
to understand it, and then she might tell the
tale and find rest. So when Patty came, time

after time to hear stories, it was often enough
in her mind to begin that one which had
coloured all her life ; not indeed changing her
outward circumstances or behaviour, but absorbing her whole thought.

" Poor darling," she would often say when
Patty had gone, scarcely knowing which darling
she meant, so strangely had the fair young girl
begun to take the place of Marie in old Lucy's
love, and almost in her fears. " Poor darling
—what a life she had in the lone old hall ; I'd
rather ha' been one of the martyrs in the picture books, than her. And how much she's
like her, when she opens her blue eyes wide,
wondering-like, full of questions and love ; and
when she sits so still and sad and thoughtful.
And yet *she* isn't married for a day, married to
the dead and lost.. But I must tell her ; my
poor old heart 'll burst if I don't tell somebody,
and I can talk to Patty as if she was my own
bairn."

Patty was indeed wondrously quick in understanding actual life ; a guileless, open-hearted child, made wise by love ; a true sister for Marie, dead in her widow's grave, so very lonely.

" Patty, lovey," said old Lucy, when she first began to tell her tale, " I *do* know a story, but I dare scarcely tell it to you."

" Why, I shan't be frightened, granny," said Patty.

" No, my pet, but you'll be so sorry."

And then old Lucy began to cry, and rock herself backwards and forwards, and very little of the tale could she tell to eager little Patty that first day. But when once it was all told, it seemed as if the child had become part of her very self, and Forester had scarcely left Mr. Platt's house after taking Patty home, before old Lucy called to see how Miss Wilson was. She had not heard of her danger and rescue, she had merely come to see and fondle her little favourite, and perhaps to talk awhile of those past years which Lucy seemed to have brought back by telling their sad story to another. But the old woman was utterly terrified when she heard what had happened to Patty, and who had found her, and where she had been; and especially she seemed to dread the threatened interview with Edwin Forester. She had kept carefully away from the Hall for years, and scarcely knew what its new master was like.

It was not many days, however, before he visited her. He was a little above the average height, though a slight stoop almost deprived him of that advantage. He was pale and thin, with long weak hair. Indeed weakness was written on every line of his face, and was manifested in every gesture and every tone of his voice. There was a most winning kindness in his manner, a silvery sweetness in his voice, his very stoop almost seemed to have come from a habit of leaning affectionately towards those

with whom he might be conversing; but any
keen observer might have guessed that his virtues would be all akin to feebleness, and might
too easily vanish if ever vice were to become
easier than goodness.   He entered Lucy's cottage with a courtesy, a smile, an expression of
genuine pleasure that could scarcely have been
more complete if the old woman's house had
been the oft-frequented home of his best and most
cherished friend.   With perfect ease he seated
himself by her side and began to talk about
Patty's accident; and then he told her how often
and how earnestly he had longed to gain some
certain knowledge of his father, and how un-
speakably indebted he should feel to her if she
could give him any clue to guide him in his
search.   The old woman could tell him no more
than she had told Patty, and there was little
enough of hope in that.   But with his charac-
teristic love of change, glad of any excuse for
a holiday, and for any adventure that had a

little romance and no danger, firmly believing that he really wished to find his father, and that it was somehow the proper thing to do, he set out in a few days for Torquay. " I shall never have any peace," he said, " till I've tried my best, and then if after all I fail, it won't be my fault."

" Ah," said Lucy to herself, when he had left her cottage, " he must be the image of his father. Just the voice to win a lassie, and somehow mean no harm in anything. What a coaxing way he has ; but perhaps these folks that smile so much, and talk so sweet to *every-body*, don't care much more for their wives and children than they do for the people they meet first time. I half wish somebody else had picked Patty up."

Their holiday was soon over, and then the Wilsons left Leigh, and returned home to Manchester. Patty had promised Lucy that she would sometimes write a letter to her old friend, and that they would surely remember each other, not without love. But the old woman's work was done. The tragedy, in which her share had been only to comfort and bless, was no strange occurrence in such a world as ours. Hearts are breaking every day —broken by folly and by sin. Husbands and wives are parted; and they who should be bound in holy wedlock find only too often that the end comes before the beginning, and they are miserable and undone for evermore. But Lucy lived too far from the centre of the world's life of evil and vanity to be able to look with coldness, or even without acute suffering, on the lingering grief, the killing disappointment of Marie. She almost felt that on herself there rested some shadow of the guilt, which she was sure must be somewhere, to have worked such woe. So all the last years of her life had been burdened and darkened, by what to her was a terrible

mystery, never to be forgotten. And now
that she had told her story to the gentle,
thoughtful child, her very relief of spirit
seemed to produce a fatal syncope. In a
fortnight Mr. Platt wrote to the Wilsons to
tell them that old Lucy "was gone."

By that time, also, Edwin was tired of his
lazy tour through Devonshire, and had come
back to Clayton's Hall.

CHAPTER IV.

MOTHERLESS.

DIRTY and miserable enough the Manchester streets appeared to Patty and her mother when they first walked through them together after their return from Leigh. The very sparrows seemed to belong to a totally different race from the sparrows of the country; and the town boys and girls, swarming in the poorer streets, seemed more dirty and impudent than the sparrows. The din of traffic and machinery, and the innumerable blended sounds which make the roar and hum of a great city, seemed utterly bewildering after the perfect stillness of field and wood, broken by nothing louder or harsher than the bleating of sheep,

or the songs of birds, or the music of the
shallow, rapid river. The bright colour soon
faded from Patty's cheeks, when she could no
longer spend whole days in the open air
watching the fishes and the birds, gathering
wild flowers in the fields and lanes, and reading
in the cool shade of the wood. Yet she really
loved the town, its everlasting stir, its endless
stream of human life. She always took town
with her into the country; her favourite birds
and fishes and flowers were, to her fancy, busy
with such work, happy with such joy, sometimes oppressed with such anxieties as belong
to men and women. She was not shy, no way
afraid of strangers; indeed, nothing pleased
her better than to ask questions of those who
were wise enough to perceive how much the
oldest and wisest may learn even from children,
and who were simple enough and humble
enough to teach those who really wish to be
taught. But she had so often been disap-

pointed and deceived by people who made
very great professions of wisdom; she had so
often been told that little girls couldn't understand the very things she was for ever puzzling
herself about, and she had become so sure that
such an answer was only a cloak for ignorance
or an excuse for laziness, that she had given
up asking questions, and simply thought and
waited till the facts she was in search of might
come of themselves. Only with her mother
had she any real intimacy. Her father loved
her with a deep, fervent affection that he sometimes feared might be idolatrous ; but he could
never have understood her. The conventional-
isms of his religious life were as far removed
from Patty's simpler virtues as the etiquette of
a drawing-room, or the stiffness of a state-
ceremony, from the honest good nature of a
rustic. He had a notion that all inquiry was
dangerous, and that a sceptical " turn of
mind " was almost a sure token of reprobation.

He fancied that, in spite of Patty's sagacity, and gentleness, and obedience, and strict sense of honour, she knew nothing of "the great change," and must be treated as an inferior and benighted creature in all spiritual matters. He was glad, as much as possible, to forget her shortcomings, and to refrain from actually applying to her his narrow religious tests; and, indeed, he had a good hope that one day she might be "born again." But once or twice her doubts and inquiries had almost wrung from him the solemn warning which found better expression in his prayers—"Oh, deliver my poor child, if indeed she is in Thy bundle of life, from the gall of bitterness and the bond of iniquity." Patty loved her father with a most honest reverence; but she never could tell him her "experiences," or ask his counsel in the inmost struggles which every true heart must know. Like Job's friends he would have mistaken her very righteousness for sin, and her trust in God for rebellion against Him. But to her mother Patty was never reserved. The mother's shyness, her gentle spirit, her child-like simplicity, and the daughter's pensiveness and habits of quiet meditation, seemed to bring them together almost as sisters. They were scarcely ever separated in work, or thought, or rest—each seemed a part of the other's very self, the other's one true friend on earth.

But ever since Patty's birth Mrs. Wilson had been losing strength; she had come to be known as "quite an invalid," and it was only by summer holidays and avoiding all effort and excitement which were not absolutely necessary, that she could be kept alive. It was every year more doubtful how her battle with autumn and winter would end. "Creaking gates may hang longest," but even "creaking gates" cannot hang on for ever.

Not long after her return from Leigh Mrs.

Wilson had a very severe illness, from which she very slowly and imperfectly recovered. Still she did recover, and all but herself began to hope that the worst was over, and that the raw cold months had once again been conquered. Patty had been with her continually, not only nursing her, but by her mere presence imparting more comfort to the gentle mother than anything else on earth could bring. The poor father seemed utterly bewildered, as one round whom on every side great calamities were gathering, from which he could see no way of escape. So Patty and her mother clung together with that desperate love which grows ever fonder as the inevitable separation draws near.

"Patty, my love, how kind and good you are to me," said her mother; "and when you were lying on my bosom, and your little baby brother was lying cold and dead in his cradle, I wished you had died instead and that my little boy had been spared."

"Father, forgive us," she murmured, pressing Patty closer to her heart; " we know not what we do."

"Perhaps he would have helped you more, mother," said Patty, " though he could never have loved you better than I do. Besides it was natural enough for you to think most of the one that died."

" Well, my pet, I thought of father and a helper for him in his business, and that a boy is easier provided for, and many such things. But God knows best. Always try to believe that He knows best," she continued, " though I know it's often very hard for all of us ; and it will soon be hard for you, darling, very hard indeed."

She was lying on the sofa, and Patty was sitting on a footstool by her side. She drew her child's hand to her lips and kissed it ; and Patty rose without a word and sat on the sofa by her, their hands clasped together. They

could only weep and love. Mrs. Wilson was
first to speak again, for it is not those who are
nearest their dying whom death terrifies ; it is
those who are to live on alone.

" You needn't shrink from thinking about
losing me, dearest," she said ; "we shall not
love each other less, though I may go so far
away we cannot hear each other speak. But
you've been more to me, Patty, than I can ever
tell you. I sometimes think it is I who have
most to lose."

They sat together talking with strange calm-
ness of the happy past, and the future that, to
Patty, at least, would be so lonely. They had
both come to know that everything they
wanted to say to each other must be said
soon.

The slight improvement soon passed away,
and by the beginning of November Mrs. Wilson
was quite unable to leave her room, unable
even for more than one hour or two, on her

best days, to leave her bed. Patty was still her only nurse, her constant companion.

"Patty," she said, one day—one of her best days—"there's something on my mind I want to say to you; and yet I don't know whether it's well for you to know it before it comes. God grant it may never come at all."

She was silent and very thoughtful for some time, till Patty said—

"Never mind, mother, tell me some other time, when you feel stronger; or don't tell me at all, if you think that will be best."

"Ah, my darling," said the mother, "I never shall be stronger; and I'm sure you'd better know, and yet it may after all be one of my weak fancies, one of the many useless fears that have spoilt my life. But I fancy that there must be something wrong with father's affairs; he seems so perfectly bewildered when he comes into my room; so very kind, so very sorry to lose me, and yet sometimes I fancy almost relieved to think that I shall soon be in a better world. Only yesterday, when he left me, he was crying very much, and I could hear him murmuring as he was going out, 'Thank God! she'll be taken away from the evil to come.' Well, I do thank God for it," she went on, " for I scarcely know how I should bear it. It's hard enough to see pain that we cannot relieve; it must be far harder to increase it. I have often wondered, Patty, what you'll do if father's business fails."

Patty was seriously alarmed by what her mother said to her, though she knew well enough there was something wrong—some trouble that made the kind old man more irritable than he ever meant to be. We can't always help it ; but it's surely rather hard to visit our own troubles upon the innocent ones around us, as if it were possible to make our own hearts lighter by making others sad. Poor Mr. Wilson was so burdened, so entangled and

bewildered by the fast accumulating difficulties
of his position, that everything approaching to
cheerfulness seemed a personal unkindness to
himself. How cruelly selfish it was for people
to be happy, pleased with any paltry trifle,
while he was so utterly wretched and hopeless.
His prayers, too, night and morning, had often
puzzled and half-terrified his child. Her own
prayers were rather thanksgivings than re-
quests, the expressions of simple trust in the
all-providing love ; but her father often prayed
as if he were in the midst of some fierce conflict
with implacable enemies, and with a strong
effort, far enough from being wholly successful,
to submit to the irrevocable will of Him who
seemed known to Mr. Wilson only by the
clouds and darkness that are round about
Him.

"Yes, mother," said Patty, trying to master
her fears, lest she should add to her mother's
trouble and excitement, "I'm sure there must

be something that father is afraid of; he often seems quite frightened even to set off to business. What will happen to us all?—what must we do, mother?"

"Well, darling," said Mrs. Wilson, "the others seem almost provided for; but you, Patty—I've been so selfish—I've kept you all to myself, to be my little maid and friend, and now, when you'll need more care than ever, I can't stay with you at all. No, Patty, I don't even know what to advise you, except to remember what we have so often said to one another about the love of God, and the beauty of goodness, and the treasure that we may lay up in heaven, and the peace which passeth all understanding. I know you won't, Patty——"

"Won't what, mother?" said Patty, as her mother hesitated.

"Well," she went on, "you won't let father see more of your trouble than you can help,

Patty; he's getting an old man now, and he's much kinder than he sometimes seems, and he will be constantly blaming himself for having brought grief upon you; and we know he would not do it if he could help it, don't we, Patty?"

"Yes, mother, yes," said the child; "he shall never have a minute's pain that I can save him."

"And when you have to get your own living," said the mother, "even if you have to work hard among strangers, who will never trouble to notice whether you are merry or dull; and if you are ever sorely tempted to rebel against God, and to make life easier by bowing down to him who tempted Christ, you will fight against it all, darling, won't you? trying to be a good, brave girl, fearing nothing so much as to grieve your Heavenly Father and doubt His goodness; and Patty, dearest," she went on, her eyes glowing with strange, unwonted light, "perhaps I shall be able to help you still. I shall be sure to love you better when I am nearer God who gave you— I shall be sure to know better what to do to help you. I shall never be able to keep quite away from you, Patty ; and perhaps sometimes when you are sad and lonely, and when suddenly your heart beats, as bright thoughts of hope and comfort enter your soul, it will just be me whispering to your heart, and making you understand that God is dealing with you ' as one whom a mother comforteth.' 'In the resurrection,'" she said, speaking more to herself than to Patty, "'they shall be like the angels of God;'" and then again, with a faint, far-off voice, "'are they not all ministering spirits, sent forth to minister to them who shall be heirs of salvation ?'"

And then they kissed one another—a long kiss of pure, true love. Mrs. Wilson seemed at last exhausted and fell into a quiet sleep.

For an hour Patty watched her as she lay, her
face seeming to grow almost every moment
more beautiful with the peace of God. The
child gently stirred the fire, looked once again
on her mother's face, and left the room. She
was busy with one household duty or another
for about an hour, and when she came back to
the chamber her mother was calmly sleeping
still, and the darkness of evening was gathering
all around. There was no light in the room
but the flicker of the fire, which Patty would
not stir now, lest it should rob her mother of so
sweet a rest. For another hour she sat, till
the fire was almost out and the room was in
almost total darkness. Very quietly she rose
from her chair and went down for a light; she
found her father below, with the same care-
worn face, the same timid, anxious restlessness,
the same sad bewilderment which had now
become so habitual to him.

" How is mother now ?" he said.

"Oh, sleeping so sweetly," said Patty. "It has been one of her best days. She was talking to me for a long time, almost too long for her strength; but it seemed only to tire her into a calm, beautiful sleep. Come and see her, father."

They went up together with the light into the quiet chamber where Patty's mother still lay, and still lay sleeping; but the knees of the poor old man were loosened as he looked into his wife's face, and he sank heavily to the ground by her bedside, for the mark of God was upon her—the perfect peace of those who love Him—the infinite rest of those who sleep in Jesus.

"I heard a voice from heaven saying to me: Write, from henceforth blessed are the dead who die in the Lord; even so, saith the Spirit, for they rest from their labours."

CHAPTER V.

It would be useless to attempt to describe the bitter grief of Patty, and her dreadful loneliness. So long as it was possible she found a sort of comfort in stealing quietly into the room where her mother was lying so still; but it came at last, that awful, inevitable day, when men came to take her mother to her burial, and Patty knew at last that she was now left alone. Nay, she knew that she was worse than alone. She knew that her father would soon become, if he was not already, more child than herself, less able to guide himself, and she seemed left in darkness having no light. Her forebodings of coming trouble were all too well founded. The very week after the funeral, her father came home about mid-day, to tell her that he had no longer any business to go to, that he had quite failed, that all their furniture must be sold, and that till they could decide what they must do they were to live with the Rhodeses, who had been kind enough to invite them to stay at "Our House." The poor old man seemed half afraid to tell his daughter into what trouble they had fallen ; but she kissed her father, and told him God would help him, and then they quietly packed up together what few things they were permitted to take away, and set off at once to "Our House."

The Rhodeses were very kind, but with just a touch of hardness. In morals and in business they were something like those people, who physically are always in the enjoyment of rude health, and who never can by any device be made to know that you are ill, until you

have arrived at the brink of your grave. They
are perfectly certain that you only want a
little more rousing and bracing, and when a
quiet walk of half a mile half kills you with
fatigue, they assure you that what you want is
more vigorous exercise, or perhaps frequent
bathing in a moderately rough sea. Now the
Rhodeses never had failed : they had begun
life in comparatively humble circumstances, and
had had to make their own way in the world
—which they had made accordingly. They
had cut their coat, or at least would have done
if they had needed a coat, according to their
cloth. They had been just before they were
generous ; they had taken care of the pennies,
in order that the pounds might have a fair
opportunity of taking care of themselves ; and,
in fact, there was scarcely a single proverb
which could not have been illustrated by some
part of the Rhodeses' biography. And though
proverbs generally make people intensely dis-

agreeable, they had not produced this effect on the Rhodeses. When they found that they had cloth enough, they never hesitated to cut it into coats, or what might be necessary. They were not only just before they were generous, but they were generous after they were just. They were really and genuinely sorry for Mr. Wilson, and would have been perfectly willing, and even pleased, to provide for him and Patty as if they had been the nearest of their own kith and kin. But, somehow, they could hardly help feeling that Mr. Wilson had been rather a fool, because of course a man need not fail with proper care and management. Unfortunately, Mr. Wilson had cared much more for the coats than for the mere cloth they were made of, and had occasionally sacrificed justice to generosity. He was an exceedingly good-natured man, and did not seem to know that money was useful for anything except being spent. When he had made any good bargain, he simply felt that the time had evidently arrived for giving to his wife and children such little pleasures as the ordinary course of business prosperity would seldom allow. Of course three maiden ladies had no wives and children, and could never imagine how Mr. Wilson's profits could possibly be so soon exhausted. Besides, there are exceedingly few people in the world who are able to do their duty through every region of their life; they make a kind of compromise by concentrating their attention upon one point. Even the Rhodeses, feeling much too humble to hope for universal excellence, had determined that, at any rate, all their business transactions should be above suspicion. So they looked upon failure in business as a kind of index by which at once to determine a man's general character. Whenever anybody failed, of course they knew there was something wrong, for they had never failed. And yet they went to the sale of Mr.

Wilson's furniture, and bought up for him and Patty everything that they thought it would be painful to him to lose. They never upbraided him with his losses, and indeed they were so gentle and considerate, that the poor old man became more happy and cheerful than he had been for many long months. In fact, having survived two of the greatest calamities that can ever befal a human being, he began to rally, and he seemed to think that however spiteful destiny might be, his circumstances had become so desperate that it was impossible they could change without improvement.

So Patty and her father lived quietly and happily together at " Our House " all through the winter and spring. Patty, indeed, was often very lonely, for the Rhodeses were as unfit to be her companions as her father himself. If they could have known her thoughts and wishes they would have thought her a silly dreaming child, who could never hope to

make her way in such a world as this. Perhaps, too, they would have thought right; for
it is not easy for any one to make his way in
this world, unless that way should chance to lie
along the beaten high roads of common custom.
Moreover, everybody's way must necessarily
depend upon the place he wants to reach ; and
good as the Rhodeses were, they and Patty
were by no means journeying towards the same
resting place.   Patty was quite careless, almost
to a fault, of what people in business call success ; and less generous judges than the good
women who were her protectors might have
fancied that she was an idle, unambitious child,
willing enough to do nothing herself, so long as
friends could be found who would work to
keep her.   And yet, though she never murmured, and only in the gentlest and quietest
way expressed even her gratitude for the kindness of her friends, she was continually wondering how she should be able to provide for

herself, and, if necessary, for her father also. She dared not speak to her father on such a matter, for he had become quite settled with the Rhodeses, almost as if he were a child again and they were his parents, taking care of him, as in nature and in duty bound. Any scheme that his daughter might have proposed for leaving "Our House," beginning over again the stern work of life, would only have waked him out of a quiet dream to the rough realities of his position. Patty could never forget her promise that he should never suffer a moment's pain that she could spare him, and yet the life he was leading seemed a quiet enough road indeed, but one that led nowhither; not a home that she could call her own, not a castle of defence for her against all cares and woes. Any one of a thousand possible accidents might cast her friendless upon an unpitying world, and she was not even making the slightest preparation against so awful a danger. How much she longed to hear that whisper of guidance and comfort which her mother had almost promised to her with her last breath. But nothing was done or arranged, and for six of the summer weeks Mr. Wilson and Patty were at Blackpool again. It was just the same place as ever; there were the same sea and the same streets, the same sort of people, the same amusements, the same house to stay at, and the same friends to stay with; but somehow Patty was restless, unsatisfied, miserable. She felt that she had more than ever to do, while she was doing less than ever; and the sea, reflecting her own mood, seemed to her only the emblem of boundless dangers and everlasting restlessness. So she was glad when her visit was over, and she could return once more to the kind-hearted Rhodeses and the peaceful monotony of "Our House."

When the nights were just beginning to get long and cosy again, when it began to be necessary to have the lamps lighted even for the Rhodeses' early tea, and when Patty had long evenings for reading and thinking, with the curtains drawn quite close, and with such a warm and sparkling fire as only people in the north of England know how to make—just about the middle of October, there came two visitors from London to " Our House ;" a gentleman and his wife, married for some eighteen years, but with no children. The gentleman had come to know the Rhodeses by some business transactions in which they had a common interest, and which had been of a kind to test and prove each other's strict integrity and chivalrous honour. For a long time they had paid each other a yearly visit, and Mr. Wilson and Patty had now become so completely members of the family in which they were staying, that their presence could be no sort of reason for deferring, even for a day, the visit of Mr. and Mrs. Carlisle. So they came, as I

have said, about the middle of October. They
were exceedingly cheerful people, within the
limits of becoming mirth, and dotingly fond of
each other.   Many young ladies who were considerably more than half as old as Mrs. Carlisle,
and whose affections, however gushing and sincere, had as yet been cruelly unrequited, had
been heard to remark with a sneer that Mr.
and Mrs. Carlisle were *ridiculously* fond of one
another.   Indeed, there was a freshness in their
mutual love, which seemed able to defy all
time and change.   They kissed one another
(though Mr. Carlisle must have been forty, if
he was a day) with the most undisguised pleasure, and seemed to find as much delight in
taking walks with one another as if they were
really lovers, which very likely they were.
Nevertheless it seemed rather odd and silly to
those who had plenty of lovers, but who were
as far off as ever from having a husband.
There was, however, one little trouble ; it might

almost be called a great trouble, to distress this happy pair. They had no children. They could not in the least understand it; they thought they deserved a little family as well as many of their neighbours. One of their own servants, who a year after their wedding had married a man who was so poor, that he had to borrow the marriage fee of the girl who was to be his wife, had by this time a home like a rabbit-warren; while they, with all their prosperity and all their snug little fortune, had never been blessed with a single child. They did not know what to make of it. Good, simple-minded people. Mrs. Carlisle had even gone so far as confide this little trouble to her medical adviser; and Mr. Carlisle had told his minister that he had no doubt it was all for the best; but for all that, it was a thorn in the flesh. However, in spite of their wishes, and sorrows, and prayers, there was as yet no little Samuel to bless the heart of Hannah Carlisle.

It is not, perhaps, then, very surprising that Mr. and Mrs. Carlisle began to think that perhaps it was a " Providence," that just at the time of their visit to Manchester, Patty Wilson should have been staying at " Our House." They had heard from their friends the story of the old man's failure and the mother's death, and the Rhodeses had even asked them whether they knew of anything in London that could be offered to Patty, and by which, without un- happiness or any feeling of degradation, she could be earning her own living. They would be willing enough to keep her as long as she would stay with them, but they knew well that it would be better otherwise, and that Patty would be far happier and far stronger if she could feel that she was making her own way in the world and burdening nobody. The Carlisles had many a quiet talk about it when they were taking their lovers' walks together.

"Ah, Hannah," said Mr. Carlisle, "our first

would have been just about her age, if he'd ever been born, poor thing."

There was not the smallest reason to say "poor thing;" for his first had had no existence except in his own hopes, and had suffered no disappointment in not being born.

"Well, well, Johnnie," said his wife, "but perhaps he might have died, poor thing, and that would have been a worse trouble than this."

"Well, do you think you could really make a child of this Miss Patty Wilson, if we took her to London to live with us?"

"Oh, I'm sure, Johnnie, we should be very fond of her; she's a quiet, loving little thing; but after all it's a great risk. You see, dear, blood's blood; and I don't know how we might feel to Patty if little Samuel came."

They always called that disappointing baby "Samuel," though he was quite as likely to be a girl as a boy.

"But, however, dear," she went on, "I'm afraid there's not much fear of that; so you'll just have to put up with me and little Patty Wilson, if you can get her."

So they arranged, after consulting with their friends the Rhodeses, to offer to take Patty to live with them in London, partly as a companion to Mrs. Carlisle, partly as a kind of little housekeeper, partly as an adopted child. The Rhodeses urged Patty strongly to accept the offer; and she hesitated to accept it only lest her father should think that she was deserting him.

"Patty," he said one day to her, "I'm so glad to hear you're going to London; they've been telling me all about it. I shan't miss you at all, darling; I'm very happy here, and I have everything I can wish for. God bless you, child."

So that little difficulty was over. Not altogether to Patty's comfort, though it made the pleasant road in which she had been loitering lead somewhere. But nobody is quite satisfied not to be missed. When we must go away, we want to go without pain or inconvenience to those we leave behind; and yet, if they are just a little sorry, we are, perhaps, just a little glad. And after all, Patty was very thankful that she could be spared so easily. Her father had been smitten with a very heavy blow, but the blow had been so heavy that it had dulled his sense of pain; he had fallen into his second childhood, and he had become like those little ones who love any one as a mother who will feed and play with them. He was among kind friends, friends who could do far better for him than Patty, with all her strong self-devotion; and so, when their month's visit was over, the Carlisles went back again, and Patty with them, from Manchester to London.

CHAPTER VI.

AN ADOPTED CHILD—HEIR PRESUMPTIVE.

VERY few strangers, especially when they come from so large a town as Manchester, are so much surprised by the first sight of London as they expect to be. One large town is very much like another, and it is only by very slow degrees that any one can come to realize that it would take something like fifty large towns to make one London. Mr. Carlisle's house was in Islington, in Canonbury Square. So as the cab drove thither from King's Cross there was nothing beyond what Patty had been quite used to see. Pentonville and the rows of shops in Islington were not startlingly different from Oxford Street in Manchester; and Mr.

Carlisle's house was certainly neither grander
nor prettier than that which had been built
for the Rhodeses, with so much consideration
and good taste. It was, however, exceedingly
comfortable ; the rooms were bright and warm
to receive the travellers ; and if it was impossible for Patty so soon to feel "at home,"
she at least hoped that it would very soon be,
not only possible, but easy.

Mr. Carlisle had been very successful in
business, and had richly deserved to succeed.
He had a large shop in Oxford Street, and there
were many people who considered that having
a shop in Oxford Street was entirely incompatible with being a gentleman. I can scarcely
say what sort of shop it was ; perhaps it might be
called a general furnishing shop ; and Mr. Carlisle
having perfect confidence in his own honesty,
and knowing well that so far as he could secure
it, the quality of everything he sold was in
strict agreement with the price, felt sure that

there could be no impropriety in making known
that fact through the medium of advertisements.   There were, of course, many people
even in Islington, a suburb of London which is
perhaps more snobbish than aristocratic, who
were perfectly certain that no true gentleman
would ever be guilty of imploring the British
public, in the columns of a newspaper, to "furnish your house at Carlisle's, No. 378, Oxford
Street, with the best, &c., &c., &c."   But really
what is to be done in this noisy, self-asserting,
competing age ?   When everybody in a street is
shouting out at the top of his voice his own
merits and the excellence of his wares, what
customer can you possibly expect to get, if you
stand behind your counter as patiently as Lot's
pillar of salt, without a word to say for yourself ?   Moreover, Mr. Carlisle gave his customers
a security for his honesty, which was also regarded with mean suspicion in some of the
Islington circles, by ticketing his goods.   "The

price of every article," said the advertisements, "is marked in plain figures." Small profits and quick returns was Mr. Carlisle's business motto. He was exceedingly polite to all his customers, and while his sweet persuasiveness was almost irresistible, as with the utmost patience he took them from room to room, exhibiting almost everything that he thought might tempt them to become purchasers, he seemed to have the gift of perceiving the exact moment at which the unselfish attentions of a shopkeeper become too much for human nature to bear. He was in politics, if anything, a somewhat extreme Liberal, though a little toned down by his increasing prosperity. That is to say, he had a kind of vague notion that everybody has a right to something, and " what right," he would ask, " has one class of society to try to monopolise everything for itself ? " Of course, as his business increased, and especially after he bought himself a private house in Islington, he

began to understand that there is also a something to which everybody unquestionably has
not a right. In religion he was a churchman,
and living in the parish of Islington, it is
perhaps superfluous to add that he was a
good Protestant, and an " Evangelical."   " I
haven't time to go into the subject," he would
say, with charming candour, " but if England
isn't a Protestant country, Ichabod is written on
our walls." As to rationalism, to which allusion
was made by his revered ministers nearly every
Sunday, he had not the faintest notion what it
meant, except that it had something to do with
wolves in sheep's clothing, which ate the bread
of the church, and were Anathema, Maranatha.
He never read books ; " For when I get home
from business of an evening, I'm tired, you
know, and these books, though very good, are
a little heavy." He was, however, a diligent
reader of the " Record," and generally managed
to spread thinly over the four Sundays of a

month, the exhilarating contents of the Churchman's Penny Magazine. But for all that,
though he was narrow-minded to begin with,
and exceedingly uncultivated to end with, he
was far more of a gentleman than many of the
snobs who looked down upon him and his wife
with a sort of patronising contempt. Many of
them would have regarded his generosity as
reckless and preposterous folly; and though their
vanity might have been something more sensitive
than Mr. Carlisle's, as to the modes of *making*
money, they were very far indeed from knowing
half as well as Mr. Carlisle did, how to *spend* it.

For the first few days everything of course
was strange to Patty; even the Carlisles themselves were strange. They scarcely seemed to
have made up their minds what they ought to
call her, and kept hovering in a good-natured im-
becile way, between " Miss Wilson," and " Miss
Patty," and "Patty," with a decided tendency to
settle on the neutral ground of " dear." " What

an astonishing thing it is, Miss Wilson," said Mr.
Carlisle one evening, as they were sitting at
supper, "that we should ever have met with
you ; but it's very wonderful how many things
take place that we never expected." This remark was so obviously true, and implied so easy
a generalization from a universal experience, that
Patty found no difficulty whatever in assenting
to it. Indeed, she could hardly help smiling
as she paralleled the remark by an equally
sagacious answer. " You see, Mr. Carlisle, I was
staying at ' Our House,' when you and Mrs.
Carlisle came down to visit the Rhodeses, and
so in that way we came to know each other."

Nothing is harder to describe than the every-
day life of very common-place people. Shop,
politics, and religion—or shop, religion, and
politics, are the only subjects on which they
ever converse ; excepting that kitchen stuffs and
servants may impart a monotonous variety to
the cares and conversation of the womankind.

Not, indeed, that they have anything to say on these subjects beyond repeating hearsays or the universal experience of harassed matrons. But these topics furnish the stream of verbiage which seems to relieve the overburdened mind, and constitute a difference between animals and articulate-speaking men. Patty seemed at first, to the Carlisles, even more uninteresting than they themselves seemed to some of their friends; for she had completely lost, or had never acquired, the habit of talking about those innumerable nothings which are scarcely worth thinking about, and which at any rate may well be suffered to die out of thought, almost as soon as they are born into it. She and her mother had not been without their household cares. They had been obliged, like most other grown-up women, to manage servants and to give orders for dinner, and sometimes even to do the work themselves that otherwise must have been left undone, in their very moderate establishment. But they never thought it necessary to occupy half their time by talking about meat and the kitchen; and as to servants, they had sense enough to know that they were human beings with a very monotonous life, subject to all the infirmities of temper which beset masters and mistresses; and that it was no way to be wondered at if they were occasionally hard to manage and hard to please. Patty was perfectly amazed that Mrs. Carlisle could live so much in the kitchen, and overwhelm herself so needlessly with domestic cares. She was far enough from thinking such cares either unwomanly or mean; but then she thought the best work in the world only requires to be done, and she could see no advantage whatever in pottering about it all day long, not to mention the risk of spoiling it, and having to do it all over again. Mrs. Carlisle was one of those good housekeepers who go very often into their own kitchens; but when she had baked a pie,

or triumphed over the inherent difficulties of a
jelly, she never could let it alone; she would
come from the lower regions hot and red with
the pie in her hands; she would insist upon
Patty's observing how well it had risen, or how
beautifully it was browned, and she would
spend half the morning talking about the oven
or the flues, and how much better the new
range was than the old one, and what a silly
stupid creature that Jane was; and how, in
another minute, the pie would have been burnt
to a cinder if she had not herself opened the
oven door. A jelly was even worse than a pie;
for if it happened to be clear, which of course
it always ought to be, she would bring it up
and show it to Patty, as if nobody had made a
clear jelly before. "Isn't that beautiful, dear?
I don't think they could send a better jelly
than that from the pastry-cook's." Very likely
not—but to Patty's undomesticated mind, there
only seemed to be two stages in the exist-

ence of a jelly—first making it, and then eating it; and she couldn't for the life of her understand why the intervening period should be filled up with mere "jelly" conversation. She could make jellies and pies too, with which even Mrs. Carlisle could scarcely find a fault; but that lady felt in her inmost soul that Patty was rather a strange girl, and did not seem to be much interested in domestic affairs. As to servants, Patty had the most provoking habit of always taking the part of the domestic against the mistress. Not that she would have taken a part at all, if Mrs. Carlisle had not in a way compelled her, but that estimable woman had a rooted belief that all servants are in a conspiracy to aggravate and ruin their mistresses. If Mrs. Carlisle broke a tumbler, or even if Mr. Carlisle broke a tumbler, though that was much less excusable, the worthy matron was perfectly certain that nothing could have prevented the accident but a superhuman

control of the powers of nature ; but if Jane or
Betsey broke a tumbler, of course it was part
of the conspiracy, a clear proof of the total
and ineradicable depravity of servant girls. In
the same way Mrs. Carlisle could see nothing
but immodest forwardness in any little affectionate passages between the cook and the
baker, whereas it was perfectly plain to the un-
sophisticated mind of Patty, that there must also
have been similar love-passages between Mr.
and Mrs. Carlisle—that they also must have
had their little cooings and murmurings, breaking out at last into articulate speech ; and that,
until that happy day, when the progress of science
shall enable us to eradicate the distinctions of
sex, there always will be an Isaac pretending to
meditate in the fields whenever a good-looking
Rebekah is riding towards him on a camel.

While Patty was thus uninterested, or seem-
ingly antagonistic, where the Carlisles (and
especially Mrs. Carlisle) were absorbed ; she

was far more antagonistic where she was really
interested—stirred to the lowest depths of her
soul. Of the limited topics of conversation in
the house in Canonbury Square, religion was
that on which Patty had thought most
anxiously and most sincerely, and in the judgment of the Islington clergy utterly wrongly.
She was as diffident and as teachable as the
haughtiest priest could have desired ; but then
she wanted real teaching, and not empty
verbiage. She did not care to know who was
wrong ; she wanted to know what was right ;
and she had a notion that if people were
wrong they must be to that extent unhappy,
and needing great love and pity from their
wiser fellow-creatures. But the religious people
she met with in the Islington circle, and especially the clergy whom she heard always on
Sundays, and often at Mrs. Carlisle's tea-table,
seemed to think that mistake was a sin deserv-
ing damnation, and very much more dangerous

than cruelty or craft. They were mostly " Recordites ;" finding their best confession of faith, not in the Bible or Prayer-book, but in the rabid dogmatism of a crazed newspaper.

" I'm glad to see you reading that," said the Reverend Jonas Faithful, as he found Patty one day with the ' Record' in her hand, and a queer smile on her face ; " we need a trumpet that will give a *certain sound* in these times."

" Well, this trumpet gives a *certain* sound, Mr. Faithful," said Patty, with a strong emphasis on the adjective.

" Yes, Miss Wilson," said the divine ; " there's nothing here of mistiness and disguise, and the use of sacred words to deceive the trusting reader, and lure him on to perdition."

" Then you like the ' Record,' Mr. Faithful ?" said Patty.

" Yes, indeed I do, Miss Wilson ; it seems to me one of the strongest bulwarks of our Holy Church."

"I can't bear it," said Patty, with honest impulsiveness.

"Miss Wilson!" said the parson, absolutely overwhelmed with pain and astonishment; "Miss Wilson, what *can* you mean?"

"I mean that I very much dislike the 'Record' newspaper, and always feel very much the worse for reading it."

"I can't the least understand you," said Mr. Faithful, with perfectly genuine surprise and bewilderment; "how can it possibly make you worse?"

"Because it asks me to do what I know is wrong; to call ill-names; to condemn books that it advises me not to read; and to pass judgment upon ministers of the Church and laymen whom I do not know, and who are most likely to be much better people than I am."

"Ah, my dear lady, but they deny the truth—the truth as it is in Jesus," said the clergyman.

"How do I know that?" said Patty; "the 'Record' may be mistaken; Mr. Carlisle would never repeat slanders against one of his neighbours in Oxford Street because he'd heard somebody say something to his injury. Besides the 'Record' never helps to set people right, it only curses them for being wrong."

"But they *are* wrong," said the divine, "and you know what St. Paul and St. John say about such, Miss Wilson. They are anathema; we are not to eat with them, or bid them Godspeed."

"Well, then, Mr. Faithful," said the little heretic, "I won't adopt that plan; I'll go by what Christ says in the Sermon on the Mount —that we are to bless our enemies because God blesses His."

"Yes, my dear young lady," said the minister; "but we must not let one part of Scripture contradict another; St. Paul wrote by inspiration of God."

"And therefore," interrupted Patty, "couldn't have meant to contradict Jesus Christ, and teach us to curse instead of blessing."

At this point Mrs. Carlisle entered the room, and Patty was glad to make her escape, not without uneasiness, and the feeling that she had made an enemy, who might come to think that in cursing her he would be doing God service. There was no danger that excellent, matronly Mrs. Carlisle would ever venture into heresy. She had far too much to do; a person with pies and jellies on her mind can't be wasting her thought and energy on controversy. The good woman never inquired, and of course never doubted. She remained perfectly loyal to such scraps of creed as had got first posses-sion of her mind; and stuck to "what she had been used to." She was much too kind and good-natured to be a bigot, after Mr. Faithful's own heart; but she had great reverence for the clergy, and felt it very shocking that anybody

should deny what her favourite divines assured
her were the essential doctrines of Christianity.
It seemed very hard that they should go to
hell for it ; but if the Bible said so, there was
nothing for us but to believe it, "and God
knew best." It was, therefore, with much
anxiety that she listened as the Reverend
Jonas Faithful delivered his soul.

"I'm almost thankful, Mrs. Carlisle," he
said, "that you have no children of your
own."

"Eh, sir," said the lady, thinking of the
unpunctual Samuel, and wondering how it
could possibly be better for him not to come.
"Why thankful for that, Mr. Faithful? it's
a thing I've besought the Lord for more than
thrice."

"There are many prayers, ma'am, that it's
better for us should be unanswered."

"But why do you think so of this, Mr.
Faithful?" said the childless woman, to the

man who seemed to care more for doctrine than for all the human spirits in the world.

"Because I'm very much afraid, my dear Mrs. Carlisle, that your young friend, Miss Patty, is not quite sound in the faith. She seems already infected with that dreadful spirit of doubt, which 'eats as doth a canker.' Our conversation before you came into the room was to me exceedingly painful."

And then he told Mrs. Carlisle that Patty hated the "Record;" and he made her understand that her young charge was herself in the utmost danger, and would be a dangerous companion to any other. He had touched the very tenderest place in the good woman's whole nature—the love she had for the child that had never been born; a love that was growing keener, more overpowering, more strangely selfish every day. She gave poor Patty many solemn warnings; but she was too ignorant of any theology to do more than vaguely warn her. At the same time a cold shadow seemed to be creeping over her love for the girl that she was meaning to take for her own daughter; and those reverend hands, that should have had far other work to do, had sown the first seeds of distrust and mischief. Poor man! he thought *that* was a chief part of the work of those who watch for souls as they who must give account.

But as time rolled on, the dark shadows seemed to pass off from Mrs. Carlisle's heart. Patty might or might not be a heretic, but she was unquestionably a very good girl. Never had the house in Canonbury Square seemed so homelike. Never had its mistress's wants been so skilfully and so unobtrusively anticipated and supplied. Moreover, to the good old Oxford Street tradesman, Patty Wilson was becoming a pearl of great price. He couldn't explain how it was, but home was no longer home if she were missing. He could scarcely spare her for a holiday, or to visit her old friends the Rhodeses, and her father getting further and further from her continually, till it seemed that even death could scarcely make the breach wider. Mr. Carlisle knew that Patty could be more than trusted; he could see that her quicksighted love gave her a wisdom and energy far beyond her years, and he loved her with a deep, pure love.

So, about three years after Patty came to London, there was solemn consultation between the worthy couple who had brought her from Manchester.

"Well, Hannah," said the gudeman, "let's have a kiss and talk this matter over; it'll be a weight off our minds."

"That it will," said the gude wife; "you know, Johnnie, it shall be just as you please. I've always my fears about everything," she added, with a sigh.

"No, no, no, that 'll never do, old woman,"

said the good-natured husband ; "it's not to be as *I* like, but as we *both* like. If you're sometimes timid, you know, Hannah, I'm very often rash. We'd better not do it, if we think we should come to wish it undone."

" Well, you know Johnnie," said Mrs. Carlisle, with a sigh for Samuel, " there's only *that*."

" But we haven't got that," said the husband ; " and I scarcely think we ever shall. I suppose it's best for us."

A shade passed over the heart and face of Mrs. Carlisle when her husband said this. Was it not the echo of Mr. Faithful's ill-omened warning ?

" What's the matter, old girl ? " he said ; " what frightens you ? "

" Well, Johnnie, that's just what Mr. Faithful said more than two years ago ; and he seemed to think that Patty was hindering our prayers."

"Well, dear," said Mr. Carlisle, a little indignant that a stranger should come, even though a clergyman, between him and his cherished desire, and not sorry that he had a good excuse for speaking warmly without contradicting or offending his wife. "Well, dear, I don't often disagree with our minister, but I did then—I think we've more reason to know what a good, loving little creature Patty is, than he can have to say anything against her. And I'm sure I don't know what fault we have to find with her religion."

"No, Johnnie, no; not a word of fault-finding will ever come from this mouth"—whereupon Johnnie kissed it—"and I wish Mr. Faithful somehow had said nothing about it. But let us do what we so often talked of."

"Adopt her altogether?" said the husband, with honest joy shining in his face.

"Yes, Johnnie," said his wife, "but we'll

agree not to tell her so ; at least for a year or two. It will make no difference to her."

Still, the bad seed of Mr. Faithful's sowing was growing in her heart.

Nevertheless, Mr. Carlisle called the next day on his lawyer with instructions for a will. It was made with complete unreserve ; and if Patty had been Samuel himself she couldn't have been more generously provided for. There were many legacies ; one even to Mr. Faithful, well-meaning sower of evil seed— but with these charitable deductions, " Patty Wilson, our beloved, adopted child," was heiress presumptive to all the lands and goods of John Carlisle.

CHAPTER VII.

ABOUT a year after Mr. Carlisle had made
his will there was great bustle and preparation
in Canonbury Square. Wife, doctor, and Mrs.
Sawyers had all agreed that Samuel was
coming. There had, of course, been a considerable interval of fluttering uncertainty
before Mrs. Carlisle had ventured to breathe
her hopes, even into the ears of her confiding
Johnnie. Certainly there was a something—
she had her presentiments and her feelings—
and at last a mysterious consultation with her
medical man. He was a gentleman in good
practice, a general practitioner, and in special
favour with the sedater portion of the Canon-

bury ladies. He was perhaps a little too old for the young wives who had been only married a year or eighteen months, but he was exactly the doctor for such a woman as Mrs. Carlisle. He was a moderately tall man, slightly inclined to obesity, but with exceedingly well-shaped hands, such hands as nobody's pulse could be offended by. Moreover, he was a father himself; which, as Mrs. Carlisle often said, made him able to sympathise with *her*; for Mrs. Jessop had presented him with fourteen children, twelve of whom were still spared to rejoice in the growing prosperity of their worthy father. He belonged to the semi-clerical race of doctors, always appearing with black clothes and a white cravat, and above all, he was chatty and receptive. Mrs. Carlisle was one of those women who would not have given twopence for a doctor who would have found out what was the matter with her at a glance, and have prescribed the appropriate remedy in a minute.

She expected a doctor to sit down in an arm-
chair and listen till she had given him a full
and particular account of every one of her
symptoms. Moreover, she was in the habit of
diverging into numerous parenthetical analo-
gous cases : as, for instance, how Mrs. Jenkin-
son was taken in exactly the same way the
week before last, and how she thought it must
be something in the air. Now Mr. Jessop was
exactly the man to deal with a disposition of
this sort. Being rather stout, and more easily
fatigued than in his youth, an arm-chair
decidedly did him good; and when his duties
had been unusually exhausting, he had been
known to refresh himself with no apparent
reluctance with biscuits and sherry. Moreover,
he knew quite well that personal details and
inoffensive anecdotes about his other patients
relieve the tediousness of scientific explanations
or the unpalatableness of mere advice.

"Ah, well, my dear Mrs. Carlisle," he would

say, "your case is no doubt very trying and
wearing to a lady of your active disposition,
but I think we may be quite sure of setting
this little matter right in a few days. Indeed,
as you say, there is a great deal of sickness in
the neighbourhood. I never mention, of course,
the names of my patients—though I am sure
with you, Mrs. Carlisle, I need have no fear
—but I may tell you that a lady who lives on
the other side of the Square was distressed
last week by symptoms almost exactly corres-
ponding to your own ; and yet, she is now, I
am thankful to say, making the most satis-
factory progress to her accustomed health."

Of course Mrs. Carlisle knew perfectly well
who the lady thus darkly indicated was, and
her case was sure to suggest some other case
which naturally threw fresh light on her own
symptoms. Mr. Jessop would sit and rest
himself in the easy chair, and listen, and chat,
and sympathise, and indulge his patient with

precisely that luxury of illness, which ladies
who have nothing seriously the matter with
them so keenly relish. " Well, well," he would
say as he rose to take his leave, " I think I see
exactly the medicine that will suit your case,
Mrs. Carlisle, and I have no doubt that when I
call to-morrow I shall hear a very different
account of you."

But what were all previous conferences,
ordinary or extraordinary, compared with that
solemn consultation which had been rendered
necessary by Mrs. Carlisle's fluttering anxieties
as to the possible Samuel. Nothing could
exceed the worthy lady's embarrassment as she
had to reveal to the father of fourteen children
the happy suspicion that had entered her own
heart. She felt far shyer and queerer than a
young girl, for was not this indeed the hun-
griest hope that she had ever cherished ? And
what if Mr. Jessop should destroy it ? But Mr.
Jessop, of course, did not destroy it ; on the

contrary, he took an extra biscuit and a second glass of sherry, and his eye twinkled with just a spark of the waggishness of his youth, while he imparted comic consolation to his bashful patient.

"Ha, 'ha, ha, my dear old friend," he said to Mr. Carlisle, meeting him at the front door ; "you run in as fast as you can and drink a glass of sherry with your good wife ; she's got something to tell you, ha, ha, ha !" And so he giggled into his carriage, and drove over to the other side of the square.

No true woman can know that she is surely to become a mother without a strange thrill of wonder, and fear, and joy. It is the great divine mystery of her womanhood. It is the sum of all her duties and responsibilities, for to be a good mother is to be a good wife and woman. No man can know the living bonds that bind together mother and child, and the longing love that grows up in the mother's heart through the months of her waiting and preparation. The gush of fondness with which she gazes on each little garment as it is finished and laid by in its pure white beauty, the pride with which she trims the little cot where her darling is to rest in that gentle sleep that the angels watch over, the increasing purpose with which her life is filling day by day; how little of all this can any man know, even the very father himself of her child. But Mrs. Carlisle had longed, and prayed, and sorrowed for this dignity and gladness, until the lengthening years of her married life had well-nigh left her hopeless; and now that it really was to be granted her she began to fear lest it had been won by her impatience from a reluctant heaven.

And there was Patty, loving, gentle, good— their adopted child—the sunniest light in their house, what of her? Would there be room for her when the child of promise came? Mrs.

Carlisle had never put that question, as yet, even to herself; but it was shaping itself slowly in her mind, though she knew it not. She was not, in the vulgarest sense, a superstitious woman; so far as she had knowledge she was eminently strong-minded. Nothing could have persuaded her that her house was haunted, or that it was unlucky to kill a cricket. "Stuff and nonsense," she would have said; "nasty, whistling things, hopping into everything. *I'll* pretty soon tread on it, if you'll only show me where it is." But, like everybody else, she felt that when she walked in the dark she couldn't tell what she might stumble over; and, to her, religion was "the dark," or at least was dreadfully full of dark places. That God governs the world by fixed laws, if she could have been brought to see what that meant, would have seemed to her no better than not governing at all. She had been taught, and she heartily believed, that

God was for ever interfering with the ordinary
course of the world. She had read the most extraordinary narratives of answers to prayer, and
even of great institutions supported by nothing
but prayer, and she had no more doubt of their
veracity than she had of her own existence.
And yet, on the other hand, all prayers are not
answered; and if we prayed too earnestly, her
ministers told her, we might teaze God into
giving us a curse instead of a blessing. That
was *the* dark place in Mrs. Carlisle's religion—
the character of God. She could never be sure
that He would do her only good, and she was
terrified lest He should be intending to curse
her little babe for the punishment of *her* rebel-
lious impatience.

And this possible curse might easily enough
connect itself somehow with Patty Wilson.
The sensitive, eager love of a mother is ever on
the edge of direst cruelty; utter self-sacrifice
close to the darkest selfishness. Mrs. Carlisle

was far too ignorant intelligently to enter into the religious controversies of the day, but she could not go to church twice a week, in the very centre of Islington ultra-protestantism, without becoming acquainted with the orthodox slang, and soured by the spirit of persecution. Patty cared nothing for that jargon, and would never have dreamed of injuring the worst heretic in the world. When Mr. Faithful visited her foster-parents he always wore a grieved, pensive, awe-stricken expression as he looked at Patty. He never tried to teach her, to sympathise with her, and help her to fuller light. He gave her up until she should be mysteriously restored to a better mind. "I wish," he would say with a sigh, "that our young friend had more love for the simple truth, Mrs. Carlisle. But nothing's too hard for the Lord." So he kept a sore place always raw and smarting in Mrs. Carlisle's spirit, and the wound was all the more painful and irritating because she could in no rational way whatever justify that chill doubt which so often cooled her love for the gentle girl she had adopted.

Nevertheless, and sometimes even the more for her consciousness of a secret injustice, she treated Patty always with the most careful kindness ; and when she ventured to tell her of what would now so soon happen, she was quite charmed with Patty's unselfish joy and ready help.   And at last the long-expected, long prayed for day arrived.   It was the first day of December ; a bitter, blowy day, raw with sleet and hail.   But the house in Canonbury Square had been made so cosy, it might have defied far bitterer weather.   The doctor was there, more beaming and chatty and kindly solicitous than ever; and Mrs. Sawyers was there, a monthly nurse, very well recommended, and very well to be paid ; and, of course, the anxious father was there, pacing the dining-room like one of those wretched, imprisoned malcontents in the Zoological Gardens ; and at half-past ten at night Samuel was there.

Of course he was not much to look at. In fact, when Mr. Carlisle was permitted to enter his wife's room, which he did on tip-toe, with tears streaming down his honest face, and his brave loving heart too full for speech, he couldn't see his first-born at all. There was a little mass of blanket, and Mrs. Sawyers told him that Samuel was inside, but otherwise he could never have guessed it ; the baby was as hidden and mysterious as if he had been only a substance with blankets for attributes. Nature had dealt very gently with Samuel's mother, and she was very comfortable ; Mrs. Sawyers, costly and well recommended, had duly usurped the monthly nurse's throne, and the purgatory of husbands had begun.

What hardy reformer of the domestic and social condition of England will dare to lay his hand on that time-honoured institution, the

monthly nurse? Is there any living father
who has not cursed her, to the peril of his
miserable soul? Between a Betsey Prig and a
Matilda Sawyers there's scarcely a pin to
choose. Mrs. Sawyers being a very expensive
luxury in the lying-in room, was not to be
roughly handled, either by herself or anybody
else. She was not a nurse of all work; never
troubled to know what it is her place to do,
because she knows she has to do everything.
A nurse at three pounds the month can cook
seductive little dainties to tempt the patient's
appetite, she can tidy the room, she can even
help to make or alter baby-linen, she doesn't
think it indecent for her lady's husband to
come into the bed-room occasionally to kiss
his own wife; *item*, she can fetch and carry;
and, generally speaking, save trouble. She
can even put up with good cask porter and
wholesome table ale. But your nurse at six
pounds and upwards, with all manner of

laundry charges and extras, is a very different creature. She's not a cook, nor a kitchen-maid, nor a parlour-maid, nor a nurse-maid, nor a laundrymaid, nor a dressmaker, but a "lady's nurse." She asks what the lady wants, and of course rings the bell for the proper servant to get it. She has a tender stomach that malt liquor does not agree with, while her exhausting duties render the support of wine and brandy absolutely necessary. She has a large correspondence and an interesting and eventful autobiography. She has always received innumerable handsome presents from former patients, and affectionate and pressing invitations to pay them frequent visits as "a friend." In a word, she's a horrid humbug and imposition, and yet where is the reformer bold enough to put her down?

Patty would have been snuffed out at once had not Mrs. Sawyers perceived that she might be made use of to lighten her own labour. So she was allowed to sit with Mrs. Carlisle, for instance, whenever Mrs. Sawyers wanted to go out, and to hold the baby on her lap whenever Mrs. Sawyers was tired. But the poor husband was absolutely good for nothing in the eyes of the well recommended nurse. He could do nothing, and yet he would keep pottering about, coming home an hour earlier from business to see how his " old woman " was getting on, and in the hope of a quiet chat with her about that future which little Samuel had made so large and full. But he was constantly snubbed and out-manœuvred by the tyrant Sawyers, and found that even rebellion and battle could end only in ignominy and defeat.

Like many other people, Mrs. Sawyers was very anxious to speak her mind to her lady's husband, but didn't quite know how to do it. The resources of the class of society to which monthly nurses belong are but limited, and after much consideration she was compelled to fall back upon the very common expedient of saying in a very loud voice to somebody else what she really wanted to say to Mr. Carlisle. That unhappy victim had just been excluded by the tyrant from the chamber of his wife, and was wandering disconsolately along the passage to the dining-room door, when he heard the voice of his oppressor in loud dialogue with the cook.

"I never see such an indecent old man, cook, in *my* life," said the fiery Sawyers.

"What's the matter now, nurse?" said the cook; and the master, with his hand on the handle of the dining-room door, listened "to no good of himself."

"I'm used to *gentlemen's* houses, cook, where people know manners," replied the nurse. "I don't mean to have a man walking in and out of our room just when he chooses, as if the month was over. I declare he came in this morning, to say good-bye to Mrs. Carlisle,

when I was washing the infant. I'm not used
o such vulgarity, cook, nor do I wish it."

Mr. Carlisle went into the dining-room very
savage and very red, and rang the bell.

"Send Mrs. Sawyers to me," he said, "this
instant."

It was all very well to send for Mrs. Sawyers; anybody "can call spirits from the vasty
deep," but sometimes they don't come, and
Mrs. Sawyers wouldn't come.

"Tell your master, cook, that I'm busy, and
can't come," said the despot.

Mr. Carlisle, more angry than ever, sent a
second message more peremptory than the first,
which brought the lady's nurse at last to the
dining-room.

"Well, sir," said Mrs. Sawyers, "if you'll
kindly be quick, as—— "

"I want none of your impertinence, nurse,"
cut in Mr. Carlisle, with rudest interruption ;
"I just want to tell you, next time you've any

very impudent remark to make to me, you'd better make it to me direct, and not to the cook."

"I couldn't tell you were a listener, sir," said the nurse, in a tone of injured and indignant virtue.

"Listener! woman, what do you mean? You know perfectly well you meant me to hear."

"Well, then, *it isn't* decent," said Sawyers, changing her ground; "nurses has their feelins, Mr. Carlisle, and it isn't everybody that likes to be seen with her gownd sleeves tucked up, nor am I that one, Mr. Carlisle. But I can tell my lady that you're not satisfied, and that I'd better go, though she's far from well enough to be left."

Poor Mr. Carlisle saw at a glance that he was beaten. The woman could any day punish *him* by making his wife ill, and she was quite mean enough to do it. So she had her own

way thenceforward to the end of the month.
It did come to an end at last, as all months
will, and as even the race of Sawyerses must in
time. Home was home once more, with the
miraculous Samuel to make it more homelike
than ever.

At least it surely might have been so. How
could a little infant bring sorrow and division?
And yet Mrs. Carlisle never hushed her baby to
sleep on her bosom without remembering that
somebody else was standing in his way. She
did not know what to do or to suggest, but if
Mr. Carlisle should die, what provision was
made for their own child, their own flesh and
blood?

"It's very fortunate," she said one night to
her husband, when Samuel was about six
months old, "that we said nothing to Patty
about your will, and our intention to adopt
her ; things are so altered now."

"Why, you don't mean, do you, Hannah?
——" said her husband.

"Oh, no, Johnnie, of course not," said Mrs.
Carlisle, without letting him finish his sen-
tence. "I don't mean anything particular,
but, of course, there *is* a difference, isn't there,
dear?"

"But you'll make no difference with Patty,
will you, mother?" he said, feeling very per-
plexed and very unhappy, as strange thoughts
came crowding upon him.

"Well, Johnnie, when there are *two*, we
can't exactly leave everything to *one*."

They said no more just then, but when Mrs.
Carlisle had gone up-stairs to get baby to sleep,
her husband took from his desk his will, and
read it slowly over. Most certainly there was
nothing for Samuel, and that must be altered.
"I'll make another," he said, "as soon as I can
spare time, and they shall share alike, as if
they were both our own."

He put the will on the fire, and watched it while it crackled and burnt to ashes.

"I'll make another very soon," he said. "Mother seems a bit hard on Patty, though she doesn't mean it. God bless the girl."

He stood, gazing still in an abstracted mood into the fire. Again and again he wiped the tears that would flow, though he meant nothing more sincerely than to make a true daughter of the gentle girl who had so brightened his home and heart. He was still standing in a mournful reverie when his wife touched his shoulder.

"Baby's asleep, dear," she said; "aren't you ready?"

"Yes, Hannah. I've been burning the will."

"Thank you, Johnnie," she said, and kissed him; "it's a great weight off my mind."

CHAPTER VIII.

CRUEL KINDNESSES.

THERE is scarcely any step of more doubtful
prudence than to adopt a child, unless, indeed,
the foster-parents are a great deal older than
Abraham and Sarah, when Sarah laughed.
Very few people could be trusted even with
children of their own, if they had power, whenever they thought fit, to sever those bonds
which bind parents and children together. A
fit of passion, and much more the prodigal behaviour of children, or the lessening resources
of the father, would be continually breaking up
families, if families were things that could be
broken up. Very wisely, both matrimony and
parentage have been rendered indestructible,

and can only be in some degree suspended in very extreme cases, and after the most solemn formalities. But an adopted child is bound to its foster-parents neither by blood nor law. All the hopes they have encouraged it to cherish can be destroyed in a moment; all the habits they have compelled it to form can, by a single act of caprice, be rendered useless or injurious. For adopted children, there is often but a step between affluence and beggary; between a life of ease and luxury, and the sternest hardships with which human nature can be required to battle.

On the other hand, there is no stronger temptation to do injustice to an adopted child, than the birth of a genuine child of the house. Maternal love is almost as different from every other kind of affection as love itself is from hatred. Nothing can exceed a mother's self-devotion, the courage with which she will face danger, the patience with which she will endure all manner of hardships for the sake of her children. And nothing can exceed a mother's bitter hatred, and unrelenting ferocity and fiendish cruelty, when she thinks that her children are wronged, or that other people are standing in their way. Women seem too often incapable of believing that there is any genuine love at all, which is not selfish, exacting, monopolising; and to love their own children often seems to them incompatible with perfectly loving anybody else's children. So, what is an adopted child to do? If she is a naughty, ill-conducted child, above all, if she quarrels with the child of her foster-parents, there is of course an immediate and open breach; while even her gentleness and love may be too winning, and the mother may feel that the child of a stranger is stealing the affection that belongs to her own flesh and blood.

From the very first Mrs. Carlisle had doubted the wisdom of taking Patty home to their own

house.   Of course she did not go to them at
first as an adopted child ; but it was very difficult to discover in what capacity she really did
go.   Mrs. Carlisle was a woman of strong common sense, and she never could bear to have to
do with what she could not clearly understand,
and accurately describe.   If Patty had been a
servant, or a companion, or a governess, or even
an adopted child (though for that Mrs. Carlisle
was by no means prepared), the worthy matron
would have understood their mutual relation-
ships, and the duties arising out of them.   But
Patty was neither one thing nor another.   Mrs.
Carlisle did not know what to say to people
who asked about her.   Was she a niece, or was
she the orphan girl of some dear and cherished
friend, or was she a kinswoman of Mr. Carlisle's ?   No, she was none of these, and Mrs.
Carlisle began to think it was almost dis-
reputable to have so pretty a girl in the house,
when she could give so indifferent an account

of her. So, when it was proposed that she should be adopted, though Mrs. Carlisle's mind was far from satisfied, she felt that that course would at least give a sort of definiteness to their relationship, and so far make their way easier. Yet she never could give up hoping that one day her own child would come, and she could not doubt that Patty would then be in the way; nay, she had a kind of instinct, which taught her that there might arise a terrible conflict in her own heart, until she might come even to hate the gentle, inoffensive girl she was now adopting.

No such perplexities troubled her husband. He loved with a man's love, not with a woman's; with a father's love, not with a mother's. Patty had become truly a daughter to him, and no other daughter could be more dear. Children might be born to him, whom he would love with equal fondness, but they would never turn Patty out of his heart. He never analysed his own feelings; but if he had done so, he would have found that he regarded the merely *physical* relation of parent and child as consisting simply of a set of circumstances which necessitate the dependence, and care, and intimate mutual knowledge, out of which a deep, lasting, ineradicable affection and unalterable obligations spring. But the circumstances were comparatively unimportant, he thought, so long as the true affection was really produced, and the obligations of father and child recognised and accepted. *Some* circumstances had brought him and Patty together and united their hearts in bonds of tenderest love; and it mattered nothing to him that they were not ties of blood. He meant to treat his adopted daughter exactly as he would treat any other child that God might send him.

And he did treat her well; more and more tenderly after little Samuel was born: partly, perhaps, because she had become more useful to him, and his wife more occupied with a mother's cares and duties ; partly, also, because of a vague dread that a change was coming, and that he might have soon to choose between his wife and his adopted child. He knew which he must choose ; but it would be to him a bitter pang—the sorest trial he had ever known.

By what subtle power is it that spirits have their presentiments of coming evils, cruel separations, cooling love ? Long before any outward sign is given they feel that the storm is gathering, that they are falling into the power of some malign Influence, of which they can give no account, but that it thrills their whole being with restlessness and pain. In the cosy house in Canonbury Square there was this restless foreboding of calamity. Everybody felt it ; Patty, Mr. Carlisle, Mrs. Carlisle. They loved one another still ; but not without fear—fear, which hath torment. Mrs. Carlisle was seeking

occasion against Patty ; though she would
have strenuously denied it, and, in fact, did not
know it.   Mr. Carlisle felt as if he was being
dragged into a conspiracy ; that he soon would
be expected to do violence to his best and tenderest feelings ; and that, anyhow, he could
not escape inflicting cruel wounds, both on
others and on himself. Patty was simply
miserable. She was a woman, now ; sensitive—
almost morbidly sensitive—to every slightest
change in that atmosphere in which her affections lived.   Mrs. Carlisle was cooler, Mr. Carlisle was warmer than ever ; but both changes
meant the same thing, and were equally ominous
of disaster.   It is dreadful to be *pitied ;* to be
even caressed and fondled by those who can
scarcely keep the tears from their eyes while
they lavish love upon us, and who seem to say,
by every endearment, " Alas ! how soon it
must be over ; how bitter will be the change ! "

It was quite impossible that the change could

come without much cruelty and injustice.
There was absolutely no reason for disinheriting
Patty ; she deserved a child's place as much as
any child could possibly have deserved it—
though " blood *is* blood." There was no possibility of quarrelling with her, or of justifying
any unkindness towards her ; and even Mrs.
Carlisle did not mean to quarrel with her or to
be unkind. But she quite forgot how life is
filled full of implied promises, and that we have
no right to begin a course of conduct involving
the happiness of our fellow-creatures, if we are
not prepared to follow it to the utmost end.
She fancied that Patty could have a happy
home for some years, and then be turned out
of it, and be *happier* than she would have
been without those years of peace at all.
" Those years," she would say to herself, " were
as happy as we could make them, and she had
no claim upon us even for them." But Mrs.
Carlisle did not reason ; she had the awful,

selfish love of Samuel eating up every other affection, and becoming a curse to herself and everybody else. "She's older than baby," she said to herself, as she thought of Patty; "she's a sort of advantage over him in that. And I believe Johnnie loves her better than his own child. And she's *not* our own child, after all, and nothing can make her—and go she shall."

Of course when Mrs. Carlisle had arrived at this point, there was nothing left for her to do but lie in wait for the least offensive occasion of carrying her purpose into effect. What would she not have given for some burst of ill-temper or impatience from Patty? nay, she would almost have been thankful if, for the first time in his life, her husband would have treated her with unkindness. But nothing of the kind occurred; Patty was patient and Johnnie was kind, and even little Samuel grew plump and hearty, and laughed and cooed when he was in Patty's arms, as if he hadn't the smallest notion that he was in the arms of his worst enemy. Nothing is more aggravating than the persevering goodness of people that you intend to harm, and it was quite plain that Mrs. Carlisle must begin the quarrel, if there was to be any quarrel at all. Of course, when it did come, the innocent Samuel was the occasion of it. Mr. Carlisle and Patty were chatting together after supper, and Mrs. Carlisle was vainly trying to get baby to sleep ; baby, on the other hand, seemed to have made up his mind that he would not go to sleep till morning, till daylight did appear. He was screaming as loudly as if his voice had been born the first moment he himself had been expected, and had been growing stronger and stronger ever since.

"Don't you think, Hannah," said Mr. Carlisle, with a suffering tone, "that you could get baby better to sleep up-stairs ? "

Of course fathers are brutes ; or they would

enjoy hearing the shrieks of an exasperating infant.

"Oh yes, Johnnie," said Samuel's mother, "I can take him up-stairs, poor little fellow ;" and in that solemn moment it seemed borne in upon her that the hour of settlement had come. She went up-stairs, taking little Samuel with her, howling fearfully all the way, and then she began to consider how she might strike the fatal blow. And while she hushed her baby to sleep she was going through all that frantic self-justification which, in her inmost heart, she knew to be perfectly false and hollow. In about half an hour the baby was asleep, and she gave three or four impatient knocks on the floor to intimate to her husband, in the dining-room below, that it was quite time for him to seek repose, or at any rate to seek the chamber where rest and quiet sleep had often come to him. There was to be not much rest or sleep that night for Samuel's unhappy father.

"I should have thought," said Mrs. Carlisle (for every woman who is bent upon doing an injury, is obliged to pretend that she is suffering one), "that you might have heard that baby was asleep long ago."

"Why, my love," said good-natured Johnnie, "I quite thought that I heard him cry till within the last five minutes;" which was perfectly true.

"I'm very unhappy and disappointed," said Mrs. Carlisle, bursting into tears.

"Why, Hannah," said her husband, "what's the matter, old woman? You're quite tired and ill; that great, big boy is too much for you; you must try and get rid of him a bit, or he'll pull all your strength down."

"Oh, Johnnie," said Mrs. Carlisle, "I wish you loved him as much as I do."

"Well, I think I do love him as much as you do," said her husband.

"No, my dear, no," said his wife; "no man

can have a mother's feelings; and there are other reasons, Johnnie; you've been used to a child that never was a baby; you never had to bear with its poor little troubles; it came to you when they were all over, when it was nearly full grown; and now, when poor little Samuel cries, you think it a hardship, and don't seem at all to like it."

"I don't the least know what you mean," said her husband, entirely baffled by this highly figurative mode of expression.

"Well, then, Johnnie, I mean Patty," said his wife.

"Well, what's Patty been doing?" said Mr. Carlisle, who began to feel that he was drawn into the conspiracy at last.

"Doing? she's been doing nothing," said Hannah; "but you know when we brought her here she wasn't a baby, Johnnie; she did not cry and need putting to sleep, and wake you in the middle of the night, and sometimes just need walking up and down the bed-room for a few minutes. And I'm sure that's not much to do for any dear little baby like Sammy."

Of course not. To be waked up out of your first sleep, and compelled to march up and down like a sentinel in the dead of the night, with a baby in your arms, measuring the yards from your bed-room window to the fire-place, till you've walked about two miles—of course that's nothing in any woman's judgment. At any rate, to do Mr. Carlisle justice, he had never complained, and he said so.

" No, Johnnie, you don't complain; but I can see you don't like it," said his spouse, with a penetration into the feelings of the male bosom truly wonderful.

" No, of course, I don't *like* it," said Mr. Carlisle; " and I should think there is no human being who does."

" No, Johnnie, and you never will like it,"

said the wife, uttering each word more slowly and more emphatically than the one before it; "until"———and there she stopped.

"Well, until what, dear? Until I can't sleep, and want something to occupy my attention in the dead of night?"

"No, Johnnie. But I know it's Patty," she said, bursting once more into hysterical tears and sobs.

Now, there is a point at which even the best-tempered men give way—a last straw that breaks even the strongest camel's back; and Mr. Carlisle had been driven up to that last point, and upon her faithful camel, patient bearer of her burdens, Mrs. Carlisle had laid that last straw.

"Come, come, Hannah," said her husband; "stop that stupid crying about nothing. We have never had any words yet since we were married, and God forbid we should begin; but if you're going to work yourself up into

hysterics, you'll have Sammy's bowels all out
of order to-morrow, not to mention a bad
headache for yourself, and all about nothing
too. What *have* you got to complain of in
Patty ? "

" Oh no, no, no, Johnnie ! " said his wife,
" I've nothing to complain of, and it's no use
being cross with me, but I know you'll never
love him till she's gone."

Though Mr. Carlisle had of course known
for a long time that something was coming, he
was scarely prepared for this. Indeed, nobody
is ever prepared for being crashed against
a disagreeable destiny. He was exceedingly
anxious to give no unnecessary pain to his
wife, and he tried with all his power to speak
with the utmost coolness in quiet, well-mea-
sured words. What better can a man do under
such circumstances ? And yet, is there anything more completely aggravating ?

" You talk to me," said Hannah, " as coldly

as if we were perfect strangers to each other ; and I'm sure I wouldn't have said a word if it hadn't been for baby. I can't bear the thought of your loving anybody better than him."

"Well, my dear old woman," said the bewildered man, "don't I love you and baby, and all of you, as much as anybody can love ? Should I make any of you happier by making Patty miserable ? or should I love you more by loving her less ? Besides, I love her as much as if she were your own child, Hannah, and I'm very glad I do. She's a sweet, loving creature as ever made a man's home happy. God bless her ! "

"I wish she'd never darkened our doors," sobbed out Mrs. Carlisle. "We never had a word till she came."

"And has *she* brought us to words ? " said the husband. "What has the poor dear child done ? You haven't a complaint to make against her; it's all your own jealous temper."

" No, John," said Mrs. Carlisle, with strongest emphasis ; "jealous I am *not*, and God grant I may have no occasion."

" There you go," said John ; " that's the way when people begin quarrelling ; they never understand each other. I don't suppose you're jealous about *me*, old woman. I know it's all your love for baby. But we should have thought of this *before* we adopted Patty ; it would be cruel and wicked to send her away now. And where could we send her ? "

" Oh, if you will only agree that she shall go," said Hannah, hugging her husband, " you may do what you like for her, and I'm sure I'll do anything I can. But do let us have home to ourselves, Johnnie, and then we shall have no more words."

CHAPTER IX.

THE REFUGE.

No arrangement of course was made that night; but Mrs. Carlisle had won, as any woman may, who determines upon winning, That is to say, she can always get her way—if it is worth while. But is it? What if she loses her husband; makes him feel enslaved, thwarted, unhappy; makes him feel that his wife and he have rival interests, and that she means to be master? How much of a husband's heart is it worth a wife's while to sacrifice, even for the best "way" she can devise?

Mr. Carlisle had never been so miserable in his life, as he was after his wife's distinctly expressed desire that he should find another home for Patty. He could hardly look his dear adopted child in the face; he felt himself a cruel monster and, moreover, a cowardly sneak. He dare not openly tell her that something was wrong; but every word he spoke to her trembled with the grief of wounded affection. He would have given worlds to fold her in his arms, and tell her that whatever came to them he loved her with the best love any father could give. But that would have compromised his wife; and he knew that she was not really cruel, only like a tigress with her cubs. The knowledge of the great chasm between his wife and himself, which had suddenly gaped so wide, was even worse to bear than his grief for Patty. He had thought Hannah so different. He couldn't understand her. He wished Samuel had never been born.

Patty knew that she would soon have to

leave her friend's home. Nobody told her so ;
but she was not the girl to wait to be told.
She knew that such sounds as she heard in Mr.
and Mrs. Carlisle's chamber on the night of their
first "misunderstanding" had never come to
her ears before; and she was quite sure that
she was somehow the cause of the coolness and
bewilderment and inexplicable unhappiness
which was gathering round them all. She
couldn't tell what to do. Every day she read
the advertisements in the " Times," hoping that
they might guide her; but alas ! the people
who want and the people who are wanted never
seem to meet.

It was baby's birthday, mid-winter again,
and Mrs. Carlisle had invited a few friends to
tea ; and, being somewhat of the nature of a
solemn Christian festival, she had invited her
reverend friend and minister, Mr. Jonas Faithful. He was just the same as ever, plunged to
the neck in religious controversies, which would

have been frivolous and laughable but for their accursed fruits. He had fresh news to tell of the spread of Popery "on the one hand," and Rationalism " on the other." It seemed, he thought, almost as if the last times had come, and Satan had grown more vicious and malignant than ever, " knowing that he had but a short time." If there was any change in the poor bewildered clergyman, it was that he was more inclined to take refuge from the despair of the present in the large hopes and vague glories of unfulfilled prophecy. If only the Lord would come ! And perhaps He would have come, if He had not been here already— from the beginning and for evermore.

But even philanthropy itself, Mr. Faithful thought, was " baptised with the spirit of the world." The relief of distress was not now, as in better times, connected indissolubly with repentance. Education had become secular and godless. Even refuges and penitentiaries were apparently falling into the hands of men who thought more of restoring sinners to the social status they had lost than to the favour of God.

"The world is creeping in everywhere, Mr. Carlisle," said the divine; "even the people who don't deny the essential truths of our holy religion are trying to do without them."

"Ah!" said Mrs. Carlisle, filling up a pause in the clergyman's speech, "I'm afraid it is so, Mr. Faithful."

"I was talking only the other day," he continued, "to Mr. Whitehouse about his refuge."

"Does he keep a refuge?" asked Mrs. Carlisle.

"Yes," said the minister; "and I must admit he seems to be doing a good work. But he doesn't seem to care for the one thing need-ful—yet lacketh he one thing."

"Then who are those nice young women he brings to church with him?" asked Mrs. Car-lisle.

"They are the refuge girls," said Mr. Faithful ; " the——"

" The refuge girls !" interrupted his hostess,
overwhelmed with astonishment. " The refuge girls ! Do you mean the thieves and—
and——"

" Yes, Mrs. Carlisle ; it's Mr. Whitehouse's
peculiar plan. He says it's no use trying to do
people good unless you trust them. I don't
know how it will answer ; he seems quite to
forget the dreadful depravity of the human
heart."

" Perhaps his plan isn't so bad after all," said
Mr. Carlisle ; "almost anything's worth trying
with poor creatures like them."

" Well, I wonder," said his wife, " that
they've impudence to enter a place of worship
with respectable people, and sit there as proper
and quiet as if nothing had happened."

" Perhaps," said Patty, they've been reading
the parable of the pharisee and publican."

With a queer mystified look at Patty, whom he never could understand, the clergyman went on with his account of Mr. Whitehouse's refuge. It was not very accurate; but he concluded with a little bit of information that made Patty's heart beat fast.

"Mr. Whitehouse is looking for a young lady to help his wife in the management of his refuge. I earnestly advised him to get an elderly experienced matron—at least, not a day younger than fifty-five—somebody with strong will and a commanding presence, who could keep the girls in subjection. He gave me a very odd answer—'If God had blessed me with a little girl, instead of that great strapping lad of mine, six feet two in his stockings, she'd have been just twenty-one next week. She must have been like her mother, Mr. Faithful, and then she'd have had a heart full of trust and love for everybody—most for those who are in deepest need. I should have had no

occasion to seek for an assistant for Mrs. Whitehouse, then.'"

"I should be very sorry to expose a child of
mine to such contamination," said Mrs. Carlisle.

"Most people would," said the clergyman.

Patty did not care much for the rest of the
conversation that evening, for she was wishing,
wondering, planning, building castles in the
air. She felt somehow sure that Mr. Whitehouse would take her, if she asked him, and let
her try to do the work he had no daughter to
do. Would not her own loneliness teach her
to comfort others? And if she knew very
little of "the world," she had such experience
of "inner life" as only orphanage and trouble
can give. After all, sin cannot give us more
sympathy for sinners than purity and goodness
can give.

Mr. Whitehouse's "refuge" was not really

called by that name ; it had no special name at
all, indicative of the benevolent purposes to
which so much of it was devoted. It was
called "Oak Villa," was not more than a
quarter of an hour's walk from Highbury
Place, was "delightfully situated in its own
grounds," and was simply Mr. Whitehouse's
own house, to which he invited what company
he chose. It was not a gloomy, prison-like
mansion, stucco-fronted, with windows of
frosted glass, and outside blinds of massive
wood such as one occasionally sees in stables.
The girls whom he took home there were not
all dressed alike in badly-fitting blue print
dresses, with big holland aprons and bibs, and
large white night-caps. They had no livery of
misfortune there—not even a livery of shame
and penitence. Mr. Whitehouse found no fault
with other institutions ; he never presumed to
say that his own mode of treatment was the
only good, or, in every case, the best mode.

But, as he had a large house and an ample
fortune, he thought it better to do what good
he could himself, in his own way, than to pay
somebody else to do it in a different way. He
asked nobody for subscriptions, so he needed
no committee or secretary, no annual report, no
public meeting, no " charity sermons ;" and, on
the other side, he was free to work out his own
belief to its utmost practical conclusion. He
wanted to know whether what he believed was
true—whether kindness could conquer cruelty
and vice ; whether chastity could win the im-
pure to the love of virtue ; whether it was well
to kill the fatted calf for the *prodigal* child.
He would at any rate try;—so he had no
black-hole, no restraint, no elaborate system of
humiliations, no perpetual mementoes of a past
that it was degradation to recal even in
memory, which it was the beginning of salvation to forget. He said nothing against those
who strove in a sterner way to raise the fallen,

and recover the lost; but it was quite other
guidance than theirs that he followed—the
discipline of nature and of God. He had
written on the first page of his journal the
words of imprisoned Alvar, in Coleridge's " Re-
morse."

" With tender ministrations, thou, O Nature,
    Healest thy wandering and distempered child;
    Thou pourest on him thy soft influences,
    Thy sunny hues, fair forms, and breathing sweets,
    Thy melodies of woods, and winds, and waters:
    Till he relent, and can no more endure
    To be a jarring and a dissonant thing
    Amid this general dance and minstrelsy;
    But, bursting into tears, wins back his way,
    His angry spirit healed and harmonized
    By the benignant touch of love and beauty."

It would, of course, have been impossible for
Mr. Whitehouse to do the work to which he
had been now devoting many years of his life,
without the entire sympathy and active co-
operation of his wife. They had at first taken
only one poor, unhappy girl to their home; a

girl whom they had found one night on the steps of Union Chapel, Islington, weeping over a dead baby—better, far better, dead, though she would have wept it to life again if she could. Dead as it was it seemed the only thing she had in all this cold, treacherous world to love and cling to.

"Oh! lady, lady," she said, as Mrs. White-house bent over her, "look at him. My baby's dead—dead—oh, my God !"

And then she wept as if her heart would break. He was all she had. Yes, *all!* Not a penny, not a crust of bread, not a fireside any-where, for all the world's so wide, that she could go to out of the bleak air, and say "I'm at home." No father, no mother—alas! the old story of sin and woe ! No husband to take from her the poor dead baby that lay so sickeningly cold against her heart.

"Look, lady, at his poor worn arms and limbs;" and she pressed him to her bosom, as if he could still know the love that was yearning over him—perhaps he could better than ever. " He cried so all day, till I thought somebody was driving sharp nails into my head ; but I had nothing to give him, lady. It was striking seven when I sat down here, and he was getting quiet, quieter and quieter, and it struck eight before I dared look at him. I knew what was making him so still. Oh, my God ! my God !"

Mr. Whitehouse slipped away to the corner of Highbury Place for a cab—he thought that would be better than fetching a policeman to take her to the comforts of a workhouse. He took her himself to Oak Villa instead. The inquest on the body of her poor little son was held in his own dining-room, and the poor desolate mother was the first lost sister that this good brother and his wife brought home. And now they had saved so many that they wanted help. Two or three new rooms had been added to Oak Villa, for the growing company of the "redeemed." It was a costly family; but after all not so costly as carriages and horses, and idle flunkeys, and wasteful stewards, and all the wreck and ruin of fashionable life.

To Oak Villa, then, the day after the birthday party, Patty went to offer herself to Mr. Whitehouse, to be his helper in the good work of his refuge home. She told him how she came to hear that he wanted help, not forgetting to explain that she had no recommendation from the worthy Mr. Faithful. She told him how it was that she had been living with the Carlisles, and how it was that, notwithstanding their great kindness, she wished to leave them. "She knew that when they took her to their house they expected to have no children of their own; and she wished to do all she could to relieve them from any obligation which they might think they had contracted when their circumstances were so

different." Mrs. Whitehouse fully explained
to her the principles on which she and her
husband were acting ; and the means by which
they hoped to restore the unhappy women who
had fallen into shame and sin to virtue and self-
respect. There was the utmost frankness on
both sides ; and it was agreed that Mr. Whitehouse should call on Mr. Carlisle at the end of
the next week, and ask him such questions as
might enable the good parents of the refuge to
judge more accurately of Patty's qualifications.
There was no doubt, however, on either side of
the result of such inquiries.

And now, how was Patty to tell the
friends she loved so dearly that she was going
to leave them—to be almost as much a stranger to them as ever. It was a sort of relief,
and yet how bitter, to know that her ab-
sence would bring back a peace and perfect
mutual trust to the home she was leaving,
which she had been the innocent occasion of

disturbing. And yet it had been a true home
for her, so far as she could have a home, when
her mother, the only real friend with whom she
could have perfect sympathy, to whom she
could tell every thought with utter unreserve,
had been taken from her. Again and again
she tried to tell her friends the determination
at which she had arrived; but again and again
her courage failed her. She must go away and
write to them. She asked if she could be
spared for a few days to spend this Christmas
in Manchester; her father was getting very old
and very infirm—he might not live to another.

The day but one after she left them they
received the following letter :—

"MANCHESTER, 'OUR HOUSE.'
"December 7th.

"MY VERY DEAR FRIENDS,
"THE DEAREST FRIENDS I HAVE.

"I am afraid I must be very cowardly,

for I've been obliged to come all the way to Manchester to get strength to tell you what I have done, and what I am going to do. But, first of all, I must thank you both from the very bottom of my heart for all your love and care. You took me to your happy home when my home was broken up, a poor motherless girl, with a father kind and good, but dead to past and future, spared in God's great mercy the grief of regretting the joys that were gone, and dreading the evils that might yet befal him. I have been very, very happy with you— I never expect to be so happy again.

"But I know, my dearest friends—though you have never told me so—that when you took me to your home you did not expect that God would send you the darling we love so much. If you had expected that, you would perhaps not have taken me—not for want of love, but you might have thought that God sends orphan children only to those who have no children of their own. I should not like to be a burden to you, my dear, kind friends—not ever so little a burden—and you have trained me so carefully that I feel sure I can manage very well now for myself. I went to see Mr. Whitehouse the day after our birthday party, to ask him if he would take me for a helper in his home. If I can do any good to my poor, miserable fellow creatures I shall be very thankful, and I think I can. At any rate, he will let me try, and will call on you this week to ask you a few questions about me. He will be glad if I can go to Oak Villa at the beginning of the next year.

"I shall not be very far away from you, my dearest friends, and I shall never, never forget your love. I shall pray in all my prayers that God may bless you; and that the kindness you have shown to me may come down ten thousand fold on the head of your darling boy.

"I am sure you will not think me ungrateful, and I know you will still let me call your house 'home ;' but I know it is best to go—best for all of us. Good-bye, my ever dearest friends. Think of me always as

"Your most affectionate,
        "And loving, and grateful
                "PATTY."

"MR. AND MRS. CARLISLE."

Big tears rolled down the good man's face as he read the letter. He couldn't speak a word, much less could he eat a bit of breakfast. He loved Patty as he had never loved her before. He would have given worlds to keep her, and yet he loved her for going : he knew it was best for all.

"I can't speak about it now, old woman," he sobbed out, as he rose from his untasted break-fast ; "I'll get down to Oxford Street, and see if I can just work a little bit of the edge off."

"He's very much cut up, poor dear," said his "old woman," as she watched him along the square ; "but he'll get over it in time, and it's much better—it's a wonderful relief to my mind. But she's an odd child—to think of going to Whitehouse's refuge !"

Yet, even Samuel's mother went not so lightly about her household tasks that day ; and she almost thought her sight was not so good with nursing that big boy so long.

One little bit of business Mr. Carlisle did in town, and it was almost all he could manage. He astonished his solicitors by sitting in their private room for something like half-an-hour, speechless with weeping, and then in broken words dictating a short will to be made, signed, and witnessed on the spot. "I want Martha Wilson to be treated, when I die, ex- actly as if she'd been my own child—my own flesh and blood—mind you make that safe, gentlemen."

CHAPTER X.

MR. JESSOP was not the medical attendant at Oak Villa, where unhappily much medical attendance was often necessary. Wicked ways are always hard and dangerous ways, and they make even a return to goodness perilous. The fierce stimulants of vice cannot always be safely withdrawn; the very abstinence seems even to hurry on the delirium that excess had prepared. No doubt the body must be sacrificed, if there be no other way of saving the spirit from demoralizing and degrading vices; but Mr. Whitehouse thought that there might be other ways. He was a firm believer in all manner of modern doctrines; which moreover often fit themselves very oddly into old beliefs. He was sure, for instance, that when men or women are possessed with devils, they need the help of Him who was not only the Redeemer of the soul, but "the Saviour of the body," and who has bestowed the gift of healing not less on physicians than on apostles.

Mr. Jessop was not an "old fogie;" but he was not the man for Oak Villa. He was far too chatty and far too conventional. The sort of treatment which never failed to soothe such patients as Mrs. Carlisle would have driven half the inmates of Oak Villa into madness or incurable insubordination. For naturally enough they were almost all of them hysterical to begin with, constantly thinking far too much about themselves and their own symptoms, both moral and physical. The chatty Jessop would have half killed them, by encouraging them minutely to describe everything they felt, or thought they felt; and suffering them to diverge, not improbably, into numerous and sensational biographies and lengthy autobiographies. Just as the Reverend Jonas Faithful would have ruined their souls, by requiring them to spend the greater part of their time in painful and laborious self-examination, so with equally good intentions, and in a very similar way, would the amiable Mr. Jessop have ruined their health. Besides, which was of course an additional proof of his amiability, no sane person would ever have trusted Mr. Jessop with a secret. His notion of being good-natured, was imparting the greatest possible amount of pleasure to the greatest possible number of persons ; and everybody knows that that is wholly incompatible with keeping secrets. You always have to choose between giving pleasure to A., and giving pleasure to all the other letters of the alphabet ; and with such an alternative, Mr. Jessop was not the man to hesitate for a single

moment. Of course he sacrificed A. with, as it
were, a pang of delight ; and yet, after all, he
did not exactly sacrifice A., for it was one of
his rules, what he called one of " the laws of
the Medes and Persians," never to mention
names. For instance, he would never speak of
Mrs. Johnson, but he would speak of the lady
who lived at one of three houses on the other
side of the square, which was not No. 13,
nor yet No. 15, and indeed he would not
say what number it was. If by your un-
assisted penetration, you arrived at the happy
guess that it was No. 14, he would say
with a smile, " Ah, well, well, well, my dear
madam, it is really no use trying to keep
one's little secrets from a lady of such quick
perceptions as yours ; but, however, I have not
said that it's No. 14. Indeed, with me, it's a
' law of the Medes and Persians ' never to
mention names." His weak, good-natured
tongue, would have made the most important

secrets of Oak Villa the common property of
all his patients before six months were over.
Moreover, he would have been utterly shocked
and confounded by the cases which he would
have been required to treat. Doctors, like
ministers of religion, often receive strange con-
fidences, but Mr. Jessop's practice had, for many
years, been among the quietest and most orderly
of respectable Islingtonians. He had never been
a " fast " young man," and he had had very little
to do with people of that order. He had exceedingly little knowledge of " life," and would
have been unable to restrain the expression of
astonishment or horror or disgust which he
might naturally enough have felt when dealing
with patients " possessed of devils "—which
nevertheless it might have been very indiscreet
and even dangerous to manifest. In fact, he
might have thought his own reputation almost
compromised, and his private practice en-
dangered, if he had become the recognized

physician in such a household as that of Mr.
Whitehouse.

So, though they were quite intimate, though,
in fact, he had been Mrs. Whitehouse's own
doctor when her only son was born, he was
never asked to visit one of the poor, unhappy
sufferers whom the good people at Oak Villa
were trying to restore to peace and virtue.
They wanted a man of great skill and wisdom,
and with a perfect command of temper and
face and tongue. Nobody in the refuge, excepting the actual managers, the doctor and
the "divine," knew anything whatever about
the previous history of any of the young
women admitted into the house ; and they
were pledged to one another by the most
solemn considerations of piety and honour to
maintain a perpetual and inviolable secrecy.

Many of the inmates of the refuge had been
simply unfortunate. One, for instance, had
been beguiled into a marriage with a man

who at the same time had a wife living, whom
he had cruelly forsaken and left to shift for
herself in one of the colonies. The poor girl
soon found out her mistake and the incurable
life-long misery into which she had fallen ; but
she had married the villain without her parents'
consent and against their wishes. So, when it
had all come to shame, and she came to her
father's house with a baby in her arms, and
asked them to take her in once more, they
simply took her by the shoulders and put her
outside the front door ; telling her that, as she
had thought fit to make her own bed, it might
do her good to lie on it. It was perfectly well
known, on the other hand, that there were young
women at Oak Villa who had sinned quite as
much as they had suffered ; and nobody knew
out of what depths of vice and ruin Mr.
Whitehouse might have raised those whom he
was seeking to benefit. He would give no
explanation, even to those whom he asked so

far to help him, as to provide what he might
consider suitable employment for those whom
he thought he might now safely trust, away
from the gentle restraints and loving watchful-
ness of his own house. He would only say to
them, "You know that I am trying to do
what good I can to those poor unhappy girls
who have fallen into trouble. Some of them
have been very wicked, and some of them,
thank God, are as virtuous as my own wife.
I cannot tell you to which class this girl
that I want you to take belongs; for we
never, under any circumstances whatever,
reveal the previous history of any of those
whom we take into our home. If you will
take this girl into your employment, it will
be on my own recommendation. I believe she
is a very good girl, one whom you may always
safely trust, as she has always been safely
trusted with us. You will be saved even from
the passing temptation of reproaching her with

the sins of her former life, because we shall
never tell you what her former life has been.
Don't think for a moment that she comes to
you without a character, for I give her one ;
and for her own sake, no less than yours, I
would never send her to you at all if I could
not give her a good one."

Fortunately Mr. Whitehouse was not compelled to avail himself of the services of a
committee of ladies ; and it was, perhaps,
equally fortunate that his expenditure was not
under the control of any committee of gentlemen.   He did and spent exactly what he
liked.   When the work became too burden-
some for his wife and himself, he chose, as we
have seen, his own assistant.   And in the same
spirit, with no need to consider what sub-
scribers might think extravagant, or red-tapists
think conventional, he had long before that
appointed a doctor.

The doctor was a comparatively young man,

perhaps eight-and-twenty; with a good practice for so young a man, but one that by no means occupied all his time.   He was moderately tall, a little above the average height, with a very handsome face—kind, firm, wise.   His manner always inspired confidence ; his patients felt at once that they were in the hands of one who knew their case, and had a clear notion what to do with them.   Or, what is perhaps better still, they felt that they could trust him even when he did not clearly understand their case ; they were confident that he would do his utmost to penetrate its obscurity, and treat them as wisely as they could at all expect to be treated by any one who had not had time to make many careful examinations, and pos- sibly some fruitless trials of useless remedies. Young as he was, scarcely a practitioner in Islington had need of fewer consultations ; or it would be truer to say, that he was in continual consultation with the leaders of his

profession. He never could have become a mere
routinist, but as yet his practice had not so
entirely absorbed his time and thought as to
leave him no leisure for reading and experiment. Moreover, he was no mere "doctor;"
he was a thoroughly well-educated English
gentleman, with the healthiest interest in every
great social movement, and especially at home
in that obscure and fascinating region where
physics and metaphysics, nature and spirit,
body and soul meet—and in meeting, seem
for awhile almost utterly lost.   Mr. Whitehouse had first met with him, soon after he
came to the parish, at the house of the Reverend
Jonas Faithful.

"You see, Mr. Faithful," he was saying,
when Mr. Whitehouse came up to them to hear
and join in the conversation, "we medical men
see so much to make us cautious in adopting
what seem to some of us very extreme theories
of human nature and of sin."

"Well, Mr. Leighton," said the clergyman—
(Frank Leighton was the doctor's name)—"but
you yourself admit that the misery and vice of
parents is transmitted to their children."

"Aye, to be sure ; but whose *fault* is that,
Mr. Faithful ?   For instance, I know people
whose ancestors have been drunkards for several
generations back ; and it might perhaps be
conjectured that a sort of dipsomania has
become hereditary in their families.   But
surely that lessens the guilt of the unhappy
children, does it not ?"

"Yes, no doubt it must," said Mr. Faithful;
"but how dangerous it would be to confound
sin with mere misfortune or even mistake.   If
we must be in doubt about the criminality of
drunkenness, is there any such thing as crime
at all, Mr. Leighton ?"

"If you mean *unmixed crime* without any
palliation, simple moral wrong without any
physical element whatever, such a case may

exist, Mr. Faithful; but I must confess, I never met with one," said the doctor.

"I'm half inclined to agree with you, doctor," said Mr. Whitehouse; "but have you quite settled which comes first, the moral wrong or the physical? I sometimes think it must be the *moral*."

"Very possibly," said the doctor; "but *now* the complication of symptoms is not much affected by the priority, whichever side it may have been on. If we could have examined and questioned the hypothetical first man ——"

"The *hypothetical* first man, Mr. Leighton?" interrupted the clergyman. "You surely must believe that there is no doubt about the inspired history we have of Adam and Eve? Science doesn't require us to destroy our Bibles, eh, doctor?"

"Certainly not, Mr. Faithful; but our Bibles give us a very meagre account of the first sin and the first pain."

"Well, well," said Mr. Whitehouse; "it doesn't much matter. We can't alter the good old Book, even if we wished; but it is of the greatest practical importance that we should have a sound principle for our guidance in the treatment of those cases in which physical and moral symptoms seem so terribly complicated."

"What would you do in such cases, doctor?" said Mr. Faithful. "How could you and I, for instance, harmoniously visit the same patient?"

"I don't see," he said, "why there need be any discord or difficulty. I should do my best for the body, and you'd do your best for the soul. I don't see how curing the body could possibly hurt the soul, and if your treatment of the soul seemed to hinder or neutralize my treatment of the body, I'd ask you to defer it till the patient was stronger."

"And if, meanwhile, the patient *died* instead of becoming stronger—what then, doctor?"

"Well, then, I'd leave him to God, Mr.

Faithful. I should not like to run the risk of killing him, even to save the soul," said Mr. Leighton.

" Ah ! my dear sir," said the clergyman, " I should be much more afraid to leave a man's soul in danger, for the sake of keeping his poor body in the world a little longer."

Even that brief conversation made Mr. Whitehouse understand that he had found a man to his mind ; one who could truly help him in his great and good work. So the very next time one of his " family " was ill, he sent for Mr. Leighton, " to come and prescribe in a case where the moral and physical symptoms were terribly complicated." That was the beginning of a true and intimate friendship, and Mr. Leighton was forthwith included in the little confederacy at Oak Villa of wise and earnest workers for those who are deepest in need— those who are in need of goodness.

But was it altogether prudent for Mr. White-

house, with such a physician for the Oak
Villa family, to admit into the confederacy
such an assistant as Patty Wilson ?   It would
have been impossible for him to have put a
stronger temptation in the way of her affections, if he had known all her preferences and
all her longings, and what sort of ideal man he
was that her heart was seeking.   She was very
self-reliant, where self-reliance was necessary ;
but she knew quite well that there was something very much better for human beings than
self-reliance ; and that mutual dependence was
much better.   Unhappily, there are very few
men upon whom self-reliant women can depend
without losing self-respect.   Now, Mr. Leighton
was just the sort of man to win the esteem and
the reasonable love of a true woman.   After
all, what is it that the majority of women do
fall in love with, or even the majority of men ?
Shall we say, a creature of the other sex, living
sufficiently near to admit of moderately frequent

interviews ; not repulsively ugly, and who has
had the good or the ill-luck to seize some opportunity of popping the question ? Indeed, for
mankind in general, this poor list of qualifications is dreadfully extravagant. Not long ago,
though this it must be confessed is an extreme
case, a woman whose right eye had been gouged
out by her first husband, took out a summons
against her second husband for threatening to
gouge out her left eye. And people with club-
feet, or mis-shapen humps on their backs, or
blind, or totally deaf, are almost always
married. Perhaps on the whole, it is most
important for the sake of securing the per-
manence of being in love, to seize a favourable
opportunity of " putting the question." There is
not the least reason in the world why Miss A.
should accept Mr. B., which would not be
equally valid for accepting any other letter in
the alphabet. But, on the other hand, she does
not see any strong reason why she should *not*

accept him, and no other letter has happened to propose. During the temporary insanity of courtship it is immeasurably more agreeable to receive the enthusiastic attentions of a devoted lover, than the half-reluctant, matter-of-course civilities which are wrung from brothers by their sisters. Moreover, a person must be somewhere ; and surely it is likely that it will be as pleasant to keep house for a gentleman nearly of one's own age, as to keep house for papa. There will always be ties to bind husband and wife together—probably children ; certainly the responsibility of the husband for the wife's debts—or, to put it more good-naturedly, the anxiety of the husband to secure a comfortable home. Surely that's quite enough. If husband and wife are both intelligent, with very many pursuits and objects of desire in common, so much the better. But such advantages seem to be considered rather the ornaments of married life, than the very stuff it is made of.

But Patty was not exactly a girl to fall weakly in love, and hurry on as fast as possible to matrimony. What she wanted was true fellowship, the union of kindred spirits ; and whether that fellowship took the form of marriage or not, was to her a matter of comparative indifference. Marriage, she thought, was pure, genuine, thorough friendship, with certain common interests and duties and experiences in addition ; and of these components she thought the friendship very far the most valuable. It was quite impossible that she and Mr. Leighton should often meet, and be occupied with different parts of the same great and difficult work, without becoming friends ; and for Patty that was enough. They found that all their lives they had been thinking the same thoughts, and fighting their way to the same results. They had sympathy with each other, not merely on the uppermost surface of their lives, but in the region of profoundest

realities, strongest beliefs and worthiest aspirations and efforts. Perhaps it was because they
were so perfectly suited to make each other
happy that they never thought about marrying
at all ; or, at any rate, if they thought about it
they did not do it. They were friends. Mr.
Leighton had yet to achieve success ; and for
Patty, nothing seemed more impossible than
that she should ever go away from Oak Villa.
And yet there had been a time when Patty
was not there ; and if Mr. Leighton had only
thought seriously about it, it might have been
as well to guard against any possibility of
losing her. Generally speaking, it does not
much matter if you lose a girl by waiting for
her two or three years ; there are plenty more
to be found quite as good. But every man
is not a Frank Leighton and every woman is
not a Patty Wilson ; and when two such people
meet, it is wise not to separate if they can
help it.

For, suppose any one *were* to come to Oak Villa and offer to take Patty away and give her a home of her own, and give her all the dignity and happiness of matronly life, what would she be likely to say to him? Of course she could not say she was waiting for Mr. Leighton. And was she not very often lonely with good Mr. Whitehouse and his wife? The position of a hired servant, even in those very rare cases in which the service is dignified and the remuneration ample, is not, after all, the position with which any woman can feel perfectly satisfied. Might she not be at any moment dismissed? and would she be willing then to thrust herself upon the kindness of Mr. and Mrs. Carlisle, or the hospitality of "Our House"? And that was by no means all. Patty wanted to be bound to people by indissoluble bonds; and bonds, moreover, if it were possible, not wholly of her own choosing. She longed for kindred, those to love and care

for who should be, as it were, her own flesh
and blood. Just as Mrs. Carlisle had never
been able to feel that Patty was her own child,
so Patty felt that the best of friends could
never be to her what her mother had been, or
what she had been to her mother, or what her
father and mother had been to each other.
She knew quite well that though she had no
fortune, she would *be* a fortune to any true-
hearted man; and perhaps, if anybody she could
believe in were really to ask her to be his wife,
she might not say no. And why did not Mr.
Leighton remember that there are some men
who can make women believe so very much,
though they mean so very little?

There was a patient of his, for instance, from
the country; a tall, weak, confiding, coaxing
sort of person. He was from the neighbourhood of Manchester; not fabulously rich, but
in a very good social position, living, as was
supposed, on his own estate, and by no means

condemned to that hard struggle for life which is to so many young men their first and bitterest experience. He was a great puzzle to Mr. Leighton, who was not quite sure which of his virtues were really virtues, and which were weaknesses and vice. The young man had been run over in the street almost opposite the doctor's door ; and the doctor had taken him in, till he should be able to bear the journey to his own home. He was not very seriously hurt, and was indeed very soon quite able to go home ; but he seemed to enjoy staying with Mr. Leighton, and he found no difficulty in making himself an agreeable companion. He had come, therefore, to be rather a boarder in the doctor's house than a patient. He seemed to be interested in everything that interested his host, even in the progress of medical science and surgical skill. He seemed yet more deeply interested in every social movement, every new scheme for rendering human beings happier and better. And yet somehow Mr. Leighton could not quite admire him, as he often fancied he ought to do. It seems necessary to the perfection of a man's character that he should have a fair share of aversions and hatreds. Being deeply interested in *everything* often amounts to being *genuinely* interested in nothing. Universal sympathy may be mere sentimentalism or even affectation, and at any rate the due *proportions* of feelings must be maintained. A dead donkey may be a very touching spectacle, but surely it is scarcely so worthy of our tears as the dead mother of orphan children. Besides, Mr. Leighton was never able to discover that his guest had anything better to offer than pity, as the remedy for those many terrible evils with which he appeared so deeply to sympathize. He never *did* anything to lessen them, though he was often so profoundly anxious that somebody else would do something to lessen them; or

that at any rate they would get lessened, and
with as much rapidity as possible finally dis-
appear. The doctor was sometimes afraid that
his patient was no better than a mere idler ;
who found it rather less exhausting, especially
after an accident, to manifest a boundless sympathy for all his fellow creatures, than to be
coldly out of harmony with the man upon
whose society he had become dependent. And
perhaps the doctor wasn't far wrong. His
guest *was* an idler ; that was, to begin with,
his peculiar form of selfishness. He was immeasurably too lazy even to take care of his
own interests. He seemed to think that life
was no way more serious than lying on your
back in a boat on some sunny day, floating
down with the current, just exerting yourself
now and then sufficiently to pull to shore and
take some friend on board, just to lie on *his*
back and help you to do nothing. Like people
who sit in boats, and suffer them to go where

they will, or where the tide can carry them, so
did the doctor's guest and his fellow idlers find
themselves not seldom aground, and their boat
in danger of being upset; and then each idler
was sure to accuse the other of being the cause
of the accident. Or sometimes he would find
himself hurried on to utmost danger, compelled to struggle in some grim life and death
encounter, and for his own preservation would
change the selfishness of idleness into the
selfishness of cruelty. And then when it was
all over, he would just lazily lie down, and
bask in the warmest sunshine he could find,
exactly as if nothing had happened, and find
himself in the most delightful sympathy with
all mankind. " Let me alone," he seemed to be
saying to everybody; " or rather let us make
one another as cozy and comfortable as we
can; I don't like the bother of quarrelling with
anybody if I can help it, but of course if you
get in my way and won't come out of it, I

shall have to do what I can to knock you out
of it." Idleness, after all, is a much more
malignant devil than he is often taken for.

The doctor's guest was Edwin Marie Forester;
and, though he didn't know it, he had come to
London to meet the pretty little girl whom he
had found lying on the bridge above the reservoirs at Leigh. London is, perhaps, the biggest
contradiction in all the universe, combining in
itself all manner of opposites. It is the densest
crowd, and the loneliest wilderness, in all the
world; the place where it is, above all others,
the hardest to meet, and the hardest not to
meet. Go to meet A. B. in London, and you
may wander from Bethnal Green to Brompton,
and never see him. Go to London with a firm
conviction that A. B. is in the Highlands, and
you stumble upon him in the middle of Cheap-
side. Everybody, who is anybody at all, has
to come to London, sometimes; and you'll see
your friends oftener by living there, even

though their home be in Lancashire or Yorkshire, than you would by living in the next village.

So Forester, expecting nothing less than to meet Patty, really did meet her at Mr. Leighton's house. She had come with some message from the household at Oak Villa, and was chatting comfortably with the doctor, when Forester came back from a stroll to the West End, and, knowing of no visitor, walked as usual into the doctor's room. He was apologising, and retiring ; but Patty looked so hard at him, and he felt so sure he had seen a face like hers before, that he stopped at the door, turned back again, and quietly sat down in his accustomed corner.

" Well, doctor," he said, " I *am* tired. My foot aches most disgracefully, considering the excellence of your surgery ; and, besides that, I could never go away without saying a word about this very pleasant surprise you've prepared for me. I feel perfectly certain—more and more certain every minute—that this lady and I are quite old friends. What do *you* think, Miss Wilson ? "

He rose to shake hands with her, with his wonderful confiding stoop, and sweet coaxing voice, and his not unhandsome face—there could be no mistake.

" Indeed," said Patty, " if I had met you almost anywhere else, I should have said you were Mr. Forester, from the Hall, at dear old Leigh."

" Well, well, Miss Wilson," he said, " let me assure you I'm no one else, even though you meet me at Mr. Leighton's house. Everybody's sure to meet everybody in London. I had my foot run over on purpose to meet you again, plainly enough."

" Well, at any rate, Mr. Forester," said Patty, " I am very glad to see you; and I am very glad to find that your foot is nearly well ; but when you know as many of Mr. Leighton's patients as I do, you will have found out that he makes everybody well."

"Then I am very thankful, Miss Wilson," said Forester, with just a twinge of foolish jealousy (for he was not at all in love), " that I happened to be run over in front of *his* door, instead of that other person's door—I forget his name—that nice, stout, chatty gentleman."

" Ah ! Mr. Jessop, I suppose, you mean," said Patty ; " but then, you know, Mr. Forester, he doesn't pretend to be a surgeon, and you ought not to expect anybody to have such superhuman humility, as to pretend to know less than he does."

" Oh, certainly not, Miss Wilson ; and I was very far from intending any offence to Mr. Jessop, whom, in truth, I like very much. But if Mr. Leighton were not present, I should tell you I do not think Mr. Jessop quite so good a surgeon as our friend here."

" But have you nothing to tell me about Leigh, Mr. Forester ? " said Patty. " I suppose it's just as beautiful as ever ; just the same view from your window as ever ; the same fields, the same river, the same wooded hill, and broad reservoirs ? "

" Just the same, Miss Wilson ; just as dull as ever. A man with the slightest pretensions to a sociable disposition may be moped to death there in a month. Though I really ought to praise the place, especially as people say that I've improved it a good deal."

" I'm sure it deserves the best praise you can give it. There is no place in the world I like so much as Leigh," said Patty ; " though I've never been there since poor mamma died."

" Then your last visit, Miss Wilson," said Forester, " must have been that summer when I found a little girl on a very dangerous bridge, one very dark night. By the way, if ever you come to Leigh again, you'll find that we have made that bridge much safer. That very summer I had iron rails put on both sides; it's a pity nobody thought of it before the poor old doctor was drowned."

And so they went on talking about old times and places familiar to both of them, while Mr. Leighton listened, half-pleased, half-displeased that there seemed to be so many bonds connecting his friend with his strange patient. In fact, he really was beginning to understand that he would not be altogether himself if Patty were to leave him; and if she went away to spend a holiday month at "dear old Leigh," she might perhaps never come back again.

Meantime Patty and Forester went on talking about old Mr. Platt and Lucy; and Forester told Patty how he had seen the good old woman buried in Leigh churchyard. He had been quite unable, notwithstanding all that he could learn from Lucy, to find out where his father had gone, after his mother's guardians had refused their consent to the marriage ; and indeed he had begun to fear that all hope of solving that mystery must be given up for ever.

"And after all, Miss Wilson," said Forester, "it may be just as well as it is. A man must make himself, and no father can save him that trouble. And possibly I should never get satisfied about my father's leaving my poor mother to such loneliness and sorrow as that which killed her in the old Hall. It's better as it is."

That nevertheless was Forester's sore point. He didn't know his father, and people would be all too ready to shrug their shoulders, and whisper to each other that there must have been dishonour somewhere, in father, or mother, or both.

Of course Forester and Patty met tolerably often, after this first interview at Mr. Leighton's house ; and somehow it is always dangerous for unmarried people to meet often, if they wish

never to marry each other. Probably Patty
did not think enough about the matter to have
a wish on either side, but she was certainly
glad to meet once more one of her old friends,
somebody who had known her before she came
to London, and who might therefore be worth
the attention and friendship even of her London
friends. Everybody finds it, if not more blessed,
at any rate more pleasant to give than to receive ; and though Patty abundantly deserved
all the attention she ever had received, yet she
could not help thinking that it would be very
pleasant if, after loving her for her own sake,
her friends in London should find she was not
altogether without the power to make some
return for those generous services that had been
so freely rendered to her. As for Forester,
this was one of those times in his life when he
was, so to speak, lying comfortably on his back
in his boat, drifting down the stream, without
taking the trouble even to row. Why not, just

for a minute or two, exert himself sufficiently to take at least one oar in his hand and pull towards that bank where Patty was standing, and take her into the boat with him ?—could he not float down the stream more cozily than ever ? Possibly not ; for in spite of arithmetic, two human beings, when they come to live together, are very widely different from twice one.

CHAPTER XI.

WHY do such people as Edwin Marie Forester ever marry at all? They are not the sort of people to make any true woman happy, and they always find marriage a dreadful slavery. Almost before the honeymoon is over they feel that they have committed themselves much further than they intended, and the very virtues of their wives increase, instead of lessening, their sense of disappointment and bondage. They are by no means what would be called bad-hearted people; if they were, they would probably be selfish enough to save women the misery of becoming their wives. Of course they are extremely selfish, but their selfishness is of the lazy sort, not the restless, busy, malignant sort ; and yet, they are probably even more mischievous, because they are much more deceitful and less dreaded than malignant and ill-tempered people. Probably they don't mean to do any harm ; but, on the other hand, they have no firm purpose to do genuine and positive good ; the one thing about which they are perfectly determined is, that never, if they can help it, will they themselves suffer any harm. Why could not Forester enjoy life at the old Hall, or in London, or oscillating between the two, with power to change his mode of life whenever he grew weary of it, without taking down to Leigh some gentle girl, whose life would be almost fastened there for ever, and at the same time his own life fastened to hers ?

The fact is, that Forester was in one of those lazy moods, in which the presence of a companion very greatly increases the delights of idleness. A human being cannot simply lie down and bask in the sun like an animal; he must transfer some part of the dignity of human nature even to his vices. There was not the least occasion for Forester to remain another day at Mr. Leighton's; but it needed much less effort to stay there than to go back to the old Hall. And, moreover, at the old Hall there would be nobody to talk to, except the gardener and domestic servants. Of course, if he could have taken Mr. Leighton with him, the change from London to Leigh would have been a mild and quiet excitement that he would very much have enjoyed. That was of course impracticable. But why not take Patty down? And, indeed, was she not a very charming sort of girl altogether, the sort of girl to make love to, and perhaps to propose to, and even to marry.

In fact, he had so often thought about her in this way, that it was becoming gradually a rather painful effort to conceal his thoughts. He very much exaggerated in his own mind the service he had rendered to her when he found her on the bridge, investing it with very far more romance than it really possessed, and persuading himself that he was a sort of champion, and that by saving her life there were certain mystic bonds between them which it would be a kind of profanity to sever. He could put all these feelings into the most charming language, and utter them with the sweetest voice. And he did sometimes, when he was walking with Patty (and he did that sometimes), bend towards her, and with a murmuring gentleness talk to her about the old times and places, and about the strange way in which he and she had been brought together. It was at such times that he felt it specially difficult not to ask her to go back with him, and to become mistress of that house to which he had brought her on the dark, wild night when he had saved her from so much danger.

Perhaps Patty was not without the suspicion both that such thoughts were in his mind, and also that he was by no means the perfect man upon whom she could depend with absolute trust. But, fortunately, we can please one another with good qualities that are very far short of perfection; and much of Forester's languor might be due, Patty thought, to his accident and the weakness and confinement to the house that had resulted from it. So she was quite prepared to be tolerant; and, in fact, had no very obvious reason to be forming judgments at all about one who was scarcely more than a stranger to her, and might soon pass out of her sight as suddenly and as completely as he did after her last visit to Leigh.

Forester was really in no position to marry a wife at all. He had very much improved

the old Hall; but then he had spent more
money upon it, or taken more money out of it,
than it was really worth.   He scarcely knew
how much he *had* taken out of it or what it
was really worth.   When he wanted money
he got it, if he could ; and when the time came
for paying it back again he got more, if he
could ; and a young man, who is nominal master
of a considerable estate, and whose own manners are not unpleasing, can generally obtain
repeated loans, especially if he can manage to
keep his borrowing moderately secret.   When
Forester was telling Patty how beautiful he had
made the Hall, and thinking how much more
beautiful it would be when she was there, he
knew quite well that it was really not his Hall
at all ; that she would come there, only to be
bitterly disappointed ; and that, in a word, it
would be immeasurably better both for her and
him if she never saw the place again.   But
then he was much too lazy to give anything

like a due consideration to subjects that were so extremely unpleasant. He knew quite well that if he proposed to marry her, and if she listened to him at all, she would trust him far too entirely to dream of asking him whether the Hall was really his, or how much he was in debt, or anything of that sort. Of course it would be better to ask him such questions : not at all less loving, and a great deal more prudent. But Forester knew quite well that she never would ask ; and, if he married her, when the truth came out, as it would be sure to come, " sufficient for the day would be the evil thereof." Or rather, to do him justice, perhaps he thought none of these thoughts. He simply thought that Patty was a very charming girl, and that he would like to be very much more familiar with her than two marriageable young people could be with each other, unless they meant to marry.

Mr. Leighton, on the other hand, was one of

those people who seem almost to be sent into
the world to be good examples. He had had
to fight his way in life from his very childhood, earning almost every penny that his
education had cost him ; and yet he had suc-
ceeded far more than Forester would probably
have even wished to succeed. He made no
sort of show, much less did he make a show
beyond what his real resources would justify;
but somehow he seemed always able to obtain
what he wanted, and he was in every respect
far more comfortable and far more independent
than Forester. If he had asked Patty to
marry him, he, too, would have been certain
that she would ask him no questions about the
fortune that he might be able to offer her. He
knew quite well that she would have no
fortune of her own, and that she would take
it for granted that any true man would *be* an
immeasurably better fortune than he could
possibly *have*. But he would never have

suffered her to become, in any degree, the
victim of her own generosity. He would have
told her, without being asked, what he could
offer her, and what chance there would be that
the comfort of their future life would never be
disturbed by the beggarly and disgusting
annoyances of unexpected poverty. He was
in all things a good, brave man ; one who
might be trusted, far beyond any promises that
he would ever make.

Perhaps, if he had had anybody to question
him, he might have found out that he really
loved Patty, and that there was no other
woman in the world that he would ever marry.
But he had never told her so, even if he knew
it ; he had felt sure that somehow or other she
would find it out without being told.   She
was so constantly in his thoughts, she was so
large a part of all his purposes, he saw her so
often, and their friendship was so uncon-
ventional and genuine, that he took it for

granted that she knew that he was only waiting to tell her his open secret until it should be the very fittest time for them to become, without the foolish, perilous delay of a long courtship, man and wife. Perhaps Patty really did take it for granted, also, and somehow knew in her heart that Mr. Leighton loved her, and that if she would wait till the right time came he would certainly marry her. If she had had a mother or a sister they would have talked to her about him; and she would have put into clear words, or, at any rate, into some distinct form of thought, what in her inmost heart she believed. But she had no mother, and her sisters were far away; and so she went on, quietly discharging her duties— undoubtedly much happier for Mr. Leighton's gentle affection, but not knowing, and scarcely thinking, to what better or higher it might come. Besides, a girl may have ever so many wishes, and hopes, and expectations; but

before a clear offer of marriage, they all fade
away into comparative insignificance. Innumerable possibilities can never equal that
one certainty. Patty was a wise, strong
woman ; not at all the sort of woman to marry
the first person who offered, as if she had no
other chance of honourable life. But she was
often exceedingly lonely ; her heart was constantly hungering for some home that she
could call truly her own. Any one of an
innumerable host of not unlikely accidents
might reduce her, if not to beggary, at least to
dependence. It was very seldom that she felt
this danger at all painfully ; but it was a real
danger, and one which the very kindness of
her friends and the comforts of her position
seemed to make more terrible. Her life was
very useful and full of good fruits ; but everybody wants to share the joy of doing good
with another, and needs the support of sympathy in those dark hours when " all seems

vanity and vexation of spirit." For there are times when love seems only to produce ingratitude, and_trust betrayal, and good itself every kind of evil.

"Do you never feel lonely here, Miss Wilson?" said Forester to Patty one day, as they were walking together under the trees in Regent's Park; "even in spite of your good and useful life your position seems to me rather solitary."

"I am very happy indeed, Mr. Forester," said Patty.

"Yes, I've no doubt of it," he replied; "you could scarcely fail to be *happy*. But I said *lonely*, Miss Wilson, and very possibly I was intruding upon your confidence too much. In fact, I was half interpreting your life by my own; I am utterly lonely a thousand times over, and always have been. I've not even a happy memory of a sunny past to bear me company. But you know my story, Miss

Wilson—a poor story without plot or characters."

" Nay, Mr. Forester," said Patty, " I am very
far from thinking it a poor story ; and as for
the plot, it seems to me that there is too much
plot, if anything, rather than too little. Have
you even found it out yourself yet ? "

" No, indeed ; and for that reason I begin to
think, considering how long I've been seeking,
that there is no plot at all, that my past
life is a very common-place thing indeed, and
that all the difference between my biography
and anybody else's is simply this, that the
first five or six chapters of mine have been
torn out and lost. But do you think, Miss
Patty, that if they had been very interesting, they would not somehow have been
saved ? "

" Well, I am not in a position to have an
opinion," she said. " The early chapters might
doubtless have been lost, because they were

utterly without interest; but, on the other hand, they might have been destroyed because they were too interesting. Poor old Lucy seemed to think they were interesting enough."

"Yes," said Forester, "she was a good old soul; and when she died I almost felt as if I had lost a kinswoman, though in truth I never spoke to her in my life until the day after I found you on the bridge."

"And did she tell you all she knew?" said Patty; "and did not that throw any light upon the mystery?"

"Yes, of course," he said; "it did throw some kind of light on a very little bit of the mystery. But the little bit was quite by itself, and therefore a useless little bit. She told me that my father and mother spent the one day of their married life in Devonshire, and so I went to Devonshire; and though I went with the best intentions, I almost felt a fool when I got there. I did not know anybody whom I could ask about my father, an unknown individual who spent a single night at Torquay more than a score of years before, and then vanished. The people were all as dumb as paving-stones, and knew exactly as much about my father as the paving-stones did. Now I don't think myself much of a hero, Miss Patty, but I know quite well that I would set off this moment for the antipodes if I thought I should find my father there ; and I must confess it puzzles me very much to know why *he* didn't set off to London or Leigh to find my mother. No, no, Miss Patty, he can't have been much of a man. For don't you see," he said, with unwonted energy ; " he must have been a fool to go through a marriage at all under such circumstances ; and he must have been a greater fool still not to carry the thing out when he had once begun it."

" Well, I think," said Patty, " I wouldn't

speak quite so harshly about your father, considering that you really know nothing about
him.   There is a good deal of common sense
in all proverbs, and 'what can't be cured must
be endured.'   I can quite understand how it
might have been a very difficult achievement
of perfect unselfishness for your father to leave
your mother alone.   If he had found out
where she was, and tried to get interviews
with her, he could have done her no sort of
good, and he would only have subjected her to
a long series of severe persecutions.   I don't
think we shall ever hear the end of the story;
but I have no doubt there *was* a story, with
a deep plot, and characters both strong and
tender.   But may I sit?" she said, for they
were close to one of the seats in the park; " I
have had a rather busy day, and am quite
tired."

"Yes, indeed," he said; "I ought to have
thought of that before.   But do you know,"

he went on, sitting down by her side, " how strange it is for me to hear anybody say *we* ? You see, Miss Patty, if I were to succeed ever so well nobody would be the happier ; and if I failed ever so miserably, thank God, nobody would be any the worse."

Patty said nothing to this, for indeed what could she say ?

"Yes, yes, you understand me, Miss Wilson," he went on ; " that's just what I mean by being so perfectly lonely, though it was a silly thing to say that I thought you must be lonely too. There must be hundreds of people to thank you, and care for you, and love you."

"Ah, Mr. Forester," said Patty, " people are thankful for very little, and so I have many more friends than I deserve. But I do feel sometimes rather lonely ; and, on the other hand, I am sure that you need not feel so lonely as you do ; it is quite impossible for

any human being to be altogether without
friends."

" Well," he said, "I wish I could believe it ;
but if I were shot through the heart to-morrow
I don't know a single human being who would
shed a tear."

He rose ;—he seemed to be, and indeed he
really was, deeply moved.   He *was* lonely, and
he pitied himself, as he thought how friendless
he was ; just as much better men might have
pitied a fellow-creature in a similar case.
Indeed he might well be moved, contemplating
his own solitariness ; for all the affection that
he ought to have bestowed upon a whole
world-full of needy, suffering creatures, he had
spent almost to the last farthing on himself.
He was for himself, the one object in the whole
universe, and he loved and pitied himself with
his whole soul.   And yet he scarcely knew
how selfish a man he was.   He thought that
he was made miserable by the unsatisfied love

of his fellow-creatures, whereas he was really
made miserable by the unsatisfied love of himself. He was actually weeping, when Patty
looked into his face.

" Don't be so unhappy, Mr. Forester," she
said, rising ; " surely a man like you may find
some way to a life of peace and joy."

" No, no, Miss Patty," he said ; " I want to
be loved, and how is it likely that anybody
will ever love me. The very first questions
they would ask me about myself would strike
me dumb. You can't think how soured I am
sometimes. I have read that poem of Hood's,
for instance, that 'Bridge of Sighs,' till its very
rhymes sound to me like the clanking of
chains. 'Who was her father, who was her
mother !' Yes, of course, that's just the
question everybody asks. And who was *my*
father, and who was *my* mother ? I don't
know anything about them, Miss Wilson,
except that they were never properly married ;

and I never dare talk to people about them, lest they should begin to ask awkward questions, and think my poor unhappy parents worse than they probably were. So, you see, I was in a manner shut out from society the very minute I was born. It would be ridiculous for me to expect that anybody would really love or care for me."

They walked slowly on together under the trees. Forester seemed to have said his say, and what could Patty answer. With her whole soul she pitied him. Had she not known his story even sooner and better than he knew it himself? Women are very suspicious, but they are always suspicious at the wrong time ; and, on the other hand, they are always stupidly confiding when their only safety would be in suspicion. Patty did not look up, but none the less for that she could see Forester's pale face, and she felt, not what *he* was feeling—nobody can feel that for other people—but what she herself would have felt, if her circumstances had been like his, and with her whole soul she pitied him.

They turned out of the broad walk into one of the quieter paths, that path which leads by one side of the Zoological Gardens to the bridge over the canal, and still they walked in silence till they came to another seat under some trees.

"Won't you sit down again and rest?" said Forester. "And let me tell you," he went on, as they both sat down together, "what I have been thinking about almost every hour since I met you again at Mr. Leighton's house. I have been thinking that it is just possible that, if there be anybody in the world at all who will care to help me out of my loneliness, perhaps you will care to do it. You know as much about the uncertainties of my history as I do myself, and somehow I can scarcely help believing that you were in a manner given to

me that day when I found you on the bridge.
Will you help me ? " he said.

Very likely Patty knew what he meant ; but
no woman is obliged to know what a man
means until he puts it into much plainer
English than that.

"I shall be most thankful," she said, " if I
can be of the least service to you, Mr. Forester."

"No, no, no, Miss Patty," he said ; "that is
not what I mean ; there is only one way in
which a girl like you *can* help me. Will
you be my wife, and come and be mistress
of my house and give me something to live
for ? "

He pleaded for himself very earnestly with
silent Patty ; with arguments which, in fact,
gained all their force from *her own* needs,
rather than from his. She had felt, far more
than he had ever been earnest enough to feel,
the want of sympathy and of a home and of
such recognised place in the world, such centre

of far-reaching good, as only honourable matrons have or can have.

No one can have a right to repeat every word that lovers say when, in the great passion of their hearts, and the very crisis of their lives, they say their utmost. In presence of Patty, as she listened, and began to gain power to speak, everything that was best and strongest in Forester rose into life, and uttered itself in the conquering eloquence of sincerity and truth. Surely the world were full of heroes if we could be for ever what we are at our best.

"I cannot answer you now, Mr. Forester," said Patty ; "you must let me write my answer to-morrow. I'm but a coward, and whatever my answer may be, there will be much that I must say and yet dare not speak. I will write to-morrow."

They separated there in the park. If they went home together, they could talk just then

on no other subject than the one which had
become so absorbing to both of them, and how
could they talk of that in crowded streets and
rattling omnibuses? And Patty, at least,
above all things wanted to be alone, to ask
counsel of her own heart, "to look before and
after," and seek for some sign to guide her
steps at this solemn crisis of her life.

She thought of the good work for which she
was living and the kind friends she had found;
indeed, in the few hours of that night all her
life seemed to pass before her in the minutest
detail, Manchester and Blackpool, and Leigh
and London. And the brightest spot of all
was the last holiday visit to Leigh with her
mother; the summer when she seemed to grow
all at once to such womanhood as might fit her
to be her mother's companion, and when she
learned to love her mother with a love as great
as if all the love of many dutiful years were
being gathered into a few short months. And

then she thought of the breaking up of the old home, and of the bitter loneliness with which she sought the shelter even of sincere friends. And then she remembered how she had lived almost as a daughter in the cosy house in Canonbury Square, and how rudely she had been made to feel the uncertainty even of what had seemed true and disinterested affection. And now, she was less dependent perhaps, but she was scarcely less solitary than ever. Even in what was now the great work of her life she had no fair and equal share, and her future happiness and usefulness depended almost wholly on those who, but a few months before, had been perfect strangers to her. Why not accept the offer of a home which should at last be her very own, from which no caprice of friends or fortune should have power to cast her out, where the whole strength and energy of her nature should find adequate work and sure recompense ? And she had seen Forester

that day as she had never seen him before.
Glorified by the earnest purpose which had
taken full possession of his spirit, his very
feebleness had seemed the sweetest gentleness
of love. She felt sure that she could trust
him ; nay, rather, she felt that she was called
to be his supporter, to charm away his loneliness, to gird on his armour like a hero's
bride, and send him to victory. How weak
and desolate they would be apart ; but together, how noble and blessed.

And Forester was thinking, too, that night,
much more earnestly than was his manner,
thoughts both good and evil. Whatever his
own languid indifference might be, it was plain
that there was no indifference in Patty ; and
that, whatever answer she might send him, she
had believed every word he had said. What
is more, and what is more wonderful, he himself believed every word he had said. For he
had been speaking, not of the past, but of the

present and future, and it was not so hard to
believe either his own good resolutions or his
hopes. The wonder was that he should have
failed to notice that every good resolution was
a mockery, and every hope a lie, which began
at any particular moment of his life, just as if
there were not a long past to be reckoned with,
before either the present or the future could be
blessed. He meant to make Patty a good
husband if she chose to accept his offer of
marriage ; but then how could he make her a
good husband when he was, in all but outward
show, little better than a beggar, and could
introduce her, not to a large fortune, but only
to large responsibilities ?   But they would
fight it out together, he thought ; she would
have more energy than he had had ; she would
repress his extravagances ; she would—not
indeed without a struggle, but still she would
somehow and in the long run—make both ends
meet : an achievement which had been hitherto

very much beyond his own power. It did not
occur to him that it was scarcely honest to
offer all this stern conflict to a young girl,
without giving her something like fair notice
of what was before her. Women are very
brave and very unselfish ; but they expect, and
they have surely a right to expect, that the
men who offer them marriage shall bring them
only the common difficulties of the future, and
not the long accumulations of past misfortune
or sin.

"I don't know," said Forester to himself ;
"she's a glorious girl, and it would be very
mortifying to be refused.   And yet, I don't
quite know whether I have been taking altogether a wise step.   I should not quite like to
have to tell everything, and spend the honeymoon in what people call making a clean breast
of it.   Girls never understand business, and
they always make a horrible fuss about
nothing ; and then, if they happen to find out

that you have a single secret, and of course
every man who is not an immeasurable fool
has secrets, they make themselves perfectly
miserable, and tell you that they have lost
your confidence and all that kind of thing.
However, I dare say I shall get through this
little affair as I have got through a good many
before.   I am not obliged to tell everything
that I know, and really it will be charmingly
snug at the old Hall.   I wonder what she will
write ? "

If he thought her letter would be a little
prosy, he very likely thought right.   He might
have been quite sure that it would be very
different from those love-letters which occasionally form part of the reports of trials for
breach of promise of marriage ; and he might
have been quite sure that it would bring him
some small measure of humiliation.   Of course
people like to impose upon their neighbours to
a certain extent.   They like to be considered

of, at least, average goodness, or even somewhat superior to the majority of their fellow-
creatures. But, then, hypocrisy is meant for
the public, and not at all for the private edifi-
cation of the hypocrite himself. When a man
is alone, masks and such like disguises are not
only perfectly useless, but extremely uncomfortable ; and Patty's letter, when it came, not
only made Forester bitterly conscious of his
own shame, but taught him that henceforth he
would have to wear his masks and disguises
always, and keep up a kind of deception at
home even more carefully than abroad. For
this was the letter :—

" MY DEAR MR. FORESTER,

" I feel, as I told you before, that it is very
cowardly to write at all, what surely it ought
to be very easy for me to say ; and now that I
begin to write, I am quite unable to tell you
half of what I feel, and I almost fear that when

you read what I write you will be tempted to think that I have no feeling at all. Is not the very tie that seems to have been binding us together so strangely, our loneliness? And does not that mean that, in this grave matter, I have no one to consult and must be my own adviser? Am I not the very last person in the world to give myself impartial counsel? And truly I feel that the step you ask me to take is of quite unspeakable importance. I feel quite certain that if we do not make each other much happier than we are now, we shall make each other very much more miserable. I have not much experience, but I am quite sure that we had better die than take this step unwisely if we are not truly meant and fitted for each other.

"As for you, I cannot doubt that you will be all you wish and promise to be, and it is that also which makes me feel more painfully how very little I can promise. But at least I will do what you have asked me; and I will do my very best to make you happy, and to help you in every great and good work that you may undertake. You know already, without my reminding you of it, that I can bring you no fortune—I wish I could. And yet if I had been able to do so, there would have been wanting one proof of the entire unselfishness of your love.

"Your kindness has made me very happy, but not with the sort of happiness that can be cheerful or talkative. Indeed, I find I am quite as unable to write what I feel, as I should have been unable to speak it. And if I wrote ever so much, what more could I say than what I put into these last lines, that I am now, henceforth, and always,

"Your own

"PATTY WILSON."

And when the letter was finished Patty lay

down and went to sleep. She was very tired ;
tired with walking, and tired with thinking—
tired with all the excitement of that day. She
soon slept and dreamed. She was in Regent's
Park again walking with Forester. She seemed
to be living the day over again in her dreams ;
for they walked along the same paths, rested
on the same seats, spoke the same words. But
as they rose at last and parted from each other,
and Patty turned to go her own way home, she
was aware of a woman, divinely beautiful,
standing close by her side, and as Forester
began to move away the woman spoke.

"Bring your lover to me, darling," she said ;
" let me look in his face and bless him."

She called Forester back, and the woman
stood close by her side till he came up. Then
she looked into his face.

" No, no, Patty ! " she said ; " take him
away. This is not the man. Surely it is not
for this man I have waited and prayed, and

come to you and him a thousand times when
you little thought who was bringing you together. No, no, Patty, put him away—I have
no blessing for him."

And as she spoke, the divine beauty of her
face seemed to pass away, and the glory that
she shone in faded ; and Forester, too, vanished
utterly, and Patty saw only her mother weeping
bitterly, and then she woke.

It was long, indeed, after that dream before
even her weariness of mind and body could
bring sleep back again. The dream, indeed,
was easily accounted for ; for Patty had been
thinking of all her past life, and of her
mother's love and death. Nay, if she had
only been able to bless the man who was to be
her daughter's husband, Patty would have believed that her mother had come in actual fact
from her glory and joy to speak to her the
words of happy omen. How could she believe
otherwise now ? As she lay awake that night

every hope she had seemed blighted, and she felt as if she had come to the very verge of some dark and awful calamity.

And Forester slept too, perhaps not quite so quietly, nor quite so soundly as usual, but still he slept; harassed by no gloomy forebodings, born of ill-omened dreams. The next morning he remembered, indeed, well enough the step he had taken, and some glow of romance still lingered about him; but he had returned once more to common sense and the easy languor of his every-day life.

"Yes, to be sure," he said, as he finished reading Patty's letter, "that's perfectly true. I should not be sorry if she had a fortune; but as she has not, we are not so unequally matched after all."

CHAPTER XII.

If Patty had only waited a day longer! If Mr. Leighton had only had courage to speak instead of writing! We little know how near we often are to the very blessedness we most earnestly desire. Somehow or other Mr. Leighton had been growing more and more jealous of Forester's intimacy with his old friend. That his guest-patient should be glad to meet once again the little girl whom he had saved some years before, that he should be charmed, and in a way surprised, to find her grown to womanhood, beautiful and good, and still almost as simple-minded as any child could be, that was natural enough. But

everybody must have found out that love is
the most meanly selfish of passions ; and it may
be doubted whether Mr. Leighton would not
have been willing that Patty should have been
neglected by all the world, if only he could
have retained her all the more completely for
himself. He did not love her any the more
because Forester had come, but he unquestionably became far more completely convinced
that he really did love her ; and often, when
Forester was speaking to her, he would watch
her face with an acutely-painful eagerness, to
see, if it were only possible, all the memories
and thoughts that were in her heart. The
human face is a very puzzling book to read ;
though, after all, Patty's thoughts at that time
were not very far beneath the surface. Mr.
Leighton was tormenting himself by half
taking it for granted that she must necessarily
be thinking, or hoping, or intending, or wishing something or other, he did not clearly

know what, but which would at any rate
destroy his own happiness, and heap up some
impassable barrier of separation between himself and her.   So every day, as the certainty of
his love grew stronger, he determined that before the night came he would tell Patty how
dear she was to him, and with what a manly
reverence he honoured her, and how unspeak-
ably grateful he would be if she would become his own true wife that they might work
their life's work together.   And then he thought
again, that perhaps there was no real danger,
that it might be premature to speak to her on
such a subject, and might defeat his own purpose.   He imagined that it must surely be
impossible that Forester should ever seem to
her a man truly worthy to be her husband,
and indeed he doubted, forgetting how the
extremes of a lazy indifference and a reckless
impetuosity often meet, whether Forester had
earnestness enough even to care to marry the

girl who was every day filling more completely the world of his own thoughts. And so another day would pass over ; and perhaps, as they were sitting together in the evening, he and his guest, some single word from Forester, the mere mention for instance of Patty's name, would raise a storm of fears and doubts in his heart, and he would again determine that before another day had ended he would know what his lot was to be. He had no need to fear ; no truer man had ever asked a woman for her love, and no one had a quicker eye than Patty to discern truth and worth. And yet he trembled, as only strong, brave men can tremble, when he asked himself in what words he should tell her how utterly he loved her, and ask her for the priceless gift of her heart and hand. No, he could not speak to her at all—he would write to her ; he could do that more calmly, and moreover would it not be more generous to her ? She could answer more calmly; and he persuaded himself that his love was far too generous even to win her love against her will, if that were possible. Surely he should have remembered that in love and war all stratagems are fair ; and in love to speak out in the purest and strongest words everything that the heart feels is of all stratagems the fairest. But Mr. Leighton was too timid and gentle in this matter that lay so near to his own interests, so near to the interests of one who had become dearer to him than himself. No, he would not, could not, speak to her ; he would write.

So while Patty was writing to Forester, and when the letter was finished, and she lay dreaming her ill-omened dream, and far on into that night, Mr. Leighton was writing to her. The letter was not long ; perhaps if it had been longer, it might have been sooner written. But even short letters sometimes need very careful writing. Mr. Leighton meant every word that he said ; he wanted to say all that he did mean and nothing more. And so he had all manner of mistakes to correct again and again, and after all he had to make a clear copy of the letter.

Knowing what he had done, and more afraid than ever that it might be too late, it was with a kind of terror that he recognised Patty's handwriting on an envelope addressed to Forester ; and with greater alarm still that he watched Forester's face while he was reading the letter. Perhaps Forester noticed the strange expression of his countenance, and at any rate he found his new secret a kind of burden. What is the use of being happy if nobody knows it? He knew that Mr. Leighton was fond of Patty ; and perhaps he had a faint suspicion that his doctor and himself had, without quite knowing it, been running a kind of race for the same prize. At any rate he soon solved any mystery that might have been involved in a letter from Patty to himself.

"I think," he said, "you ought to congratulate me, Mr. Leighton, this morning; and I am quite certain that I ought to be very thankful to you."

"Why, what service have I rendered you, Mr. Forester?" said the doctor.

"Cured my lame foot, of course," said Forester, "only you knew that before. But the best thing you have done for me was to find the little friend I saved and had lost, and bring us together again. Do you know that Miss Wilson has promised to come down to the old Hall and really make a man of me?"

"No," said Mr. Leighton, "I really did not know it; but I've not the least doubt that it will give her the greatest pleasure to visit Leigh again. I scarcely know what they can do without her at Oak Villa; she seems to me just one of those people who never can get a holiday because she deserves one so well."

"Why, what funny, prosy people you doctors

are," said Forester. " It's a very long holiday she will take. Why can't you congratulate me at once? Miss Wilson has promised to marry me."

"Well, indeed," said Mr. Leighton, "I do congratulate you most sincerely. It seems to me scarcely possible that any human being could have found a better wife."

Poor wretched Leighton; at that very moment his own letter to Patty was in the breast-pocket of his coat. It was not very easy to make the conversation cheerful; and indeed he was only meditating how he could least offensively and most naturally rid himself of his guest altogether.

"I suppose," he said, after a good deal of irrelevant conversation, " that you'll soon want to be going down to the Hall, and making all needful preparations for this great event?"

"Yes," he said, " I thought of going down in a very few days, for both Miss Wilson and

myself are so entirely free, so completely under
our own control, that there is nothing to gain,
and a great deal to lose by deferring the marriage. I shall of course leave the time entirely
to Miss Wilson; but, for my part, most decidedly, the sooner the better."

"Why I should quite think so," said Mr.
Leighton; "and, indeed, as you must leave
London in a few days, I need make no alter-
ation in my own plans for securing a very
short holiday. I shall be very glad to get
away from town myself at the beginning of
next week."

"I am sure you must need a holiday,"
Forester said; "and you may depend upon
my getting out of your way by Saturday."

And there the talk ended; and Mr. Leighton
went to his own room, tore his letter to Patty
into very small pieces and then burnt them,
and set out to comfort himself with a long day
of hard work among his patients. Work is by

far the best comfort that any one can have in trouble, at least for those who have strength of mind enough to take it; and yet, for all his work, Mr. Leighton knew quite well that he had suffered a great loss, and that, somehow, if he worked for ever, the great success that above all others he had desired, had passed for ever out of his reach.

Of course there was no reason for deferring the marriage, excepting one; and as Mr. Leighton had burnt his letter, it was impossible for Patty to know what that one reason was. So she and Mr. Forester were to be married in about three months. Mr. Leighton took his little holiday, and fought out his battle with disappointment, and gained strength even to face Patty once more, and tell her how heartily he wished for her that happiness which somehow in his heart he could scarcely help fearing she would never have. Meantime, Forester was at Leigh, taxing to the utmost his slender

purse and lessening credit for such decorations
and improvements as he thought the Hall
should have, to make it fit for its master's
bride.　It did not seem to occur to him that he
was only decorating it with debt, and that if he
could have sold it altogether and rented a
little cottage, and taken Patty there, and en-
dowed her with the sacred love of a true man's
heart, that would have been immeasurably
grander than the most magnificent palace in
the world.　If there was one thing in the
world that Forester despised it was love in a
cottage ; and indeed he was delighted and astonished, and even amused, at the childish
credulity with which people in all directions
were confiding in him, simply on the ground of
his intended marriage.　Before his engagement
with Patty his credit had been rapidly de-
clining.　Of course his tradesmen had for years
been imposing upon him, rendering to him
every half-year the most amusing variations of

his original accounts. But, though charging high interest for long credit is not altogether unprofitable, every tradesman is not unnaturally anxious to behold, at least in remote distance, some chance of ultimate payment. It was far from Forester's intention deliberately to cheat his tradespeople ; but when a profitable deception is deliberately put in a young man's way, and in a manner actually forced upon his acceptance, what virtue can be expected to resist the temptation ? The first person that Forester called upon when he went down to Leigh, after his engagement with Patty, was a builder and house-decorator, whose bill for rebuilding the Hall was only about half paid.

"I really have not come, Mr. Thompson," he said, with charming candour—and somehow or other he managed to make all his tradespeople like him, and actually help him to swindle them—" to pay your little bill, nor even to pay you the interest upon it, for I really want every penny I can get for a new investment."

"A new investment," said Mr. Thompson, with a very solemn air; "I hope you will remember old ——"

"Why, don't be frightened," said Forester, stopping him short, "I'm not going to build a palace, or start a company, or anything of that sort. I'm only going to get married, Mr. Thompson."

Thereupon Mr. Thompson relaxed, and seized Forester's hand and shook it heartily.

"Well done, Mr. Forester," he said; "I'm very glad indeed to hear it. Nothing settles a young man down into a quiet, well-conducted prosperous gentleman like matrimony, and when it's a little investment as well," he said, with a sly laugh; "why you know, Mr. Forester, love in a cottage is all very well, but it's not the kind of thing *for you*. No, no, no; an investment is very much better, and I hope you will let me have the honour of preparing Clayton's Hall for Mrs. Forester's reception."

"Why really," said Forester, "you have the instinct of a prophet; that's the very thing I came to tell you. I really want the old place to be made—well, suppose I say, to be made as handsome and comfortable as you can possibly make it, Mr. Thompson. These London ladies are used to a good deal more show than country folks seem to care for."

"All right, Mr. Forester," said Thompson; "if you will just leave it to me, you may depend upon it that nothing shall be wanting on your side of the investment."

"What a fool that fellow is," said Forester to himself, as he walked away; "and the best of it is he thinks himself so particularly knowing. He evidently thinks that I am going to marry an heiress, and that therefore he may just as well have a picking out of her estate as not. It can't possibly be any business of mine to tell him that he has found a mare's nest."

So of course Mr. Thompson set to work with the utmost energy to decorate the Hall, suggesting innumerable improvements that would never have occurred to Forester himself, and which it would have needed a very good investment indeed to justify. But he rendered to Forester far more important service than even decorating the Hall ; he set an example of trust to all the neighbourhood. Every gossip for miles round was informed of Forester's engagement to a very wealthy London lady, and those who had begun to complain of long-standing accounts, and to refuse further credit, were eager to force both credit and goods upon the man whose prospects of affluence their selfishness and stupidity had so preposterously magnified. He had no need to lie ; he found it far more difficult to gain belief for the truth. Thompson and the gossips had so determined the matter in their own minds, that every disclaimer was regarded as the mere affectation of modesty, or as an attempt to hide from them some part of the good fortune which they had firmly resolved to share.

So the works went on until Clayton's Hall was a little palace of loveliness and comfort. The gardens and conservatories were replenished. Trees were cut down where they shut out the beauty of the view, and shrubs were planted to make the walks shadier, fitter for lovers—such lovers as Patty and Forester were to be to the end of the chapter. And Forester was praised by everybody. Happy they thought must be the bonny bride who would have so generous a bridegroom. "London is a big place," said Thompson to the workpeople and gossips, "but if it can beat this, I don't mind eating my head." And Thompson's was a very pardonable pride ; and if his customer had been as good as his work, he might have congratulated himself on one of the best bargains he had ever made.

And the customer himself was as completely deceived as Thompson, long before the wedding came. It was so charming to give orders and have them executed, not only without grudging, but with the utmost alacrity; to see beauty springing forth on every side as if by enchantment; to write to Patty and tell her how the improvements were so great that she would scarcely recognise the Hall; to receive letters from her overflowing with grateful affection and loving vows. He quite forgot that he was laying heavy burdens upon her even more than on himself, which only long years of such pinching economy as he was little likely to submit to, could ever remove. He quite forgot that he was preparing for himself such bitter and vain regret, such a long series of humiliations, such a necessity for ever-thickening complications of trickery and deceit, as would turn

even the fairest paradise into a place of torment.   Nay, he quite forgot that the Hall and
everything he had was so heavily encumbered,
that there was scarcely anything in the world
he could call his own, except the memory of
sin and folly in the past, and the foreboding of
misery and shame in the future.

But there was nothing in that to put off a
wedding.   It was now the beginning of July,
and Patty and Forester were to be married at
the end of August; so that they might be at
the Hall when the wood on the hill-side would
be at the loveliest, adorned with all the ripe,
rich hues of autumn.   They were to be married in Manchester, that so they might be near
to good old Mr. Wilson, though he was too
infirm now to understand what all the bustle
and excitement could mean.   They were to
breakfast at " Our House," after the marriage
ceremony, and to spend a week or a fortnight
at the Lakes, and then to settle down at

Clayton's Hall like good, staid, old married folk. And so the weeks rolled on—six, five, four, three, two — the ever-lessening space vanishing with a solemn swiftness. At last Patty began to count, not weeks, but days. The last week had come, and nothing remained but the farewell visit to all her London friends. They were not many ; but "good-bye," for all its blessed meaning, is a word we never care to speak.

As to Mr. and Mrs. Carlisle, the parting was the less painful because they were going down to Manchester to spend a few weeks with the Rhodeses, and to be present at the marriage. Mrs. Carlisle had received the news of Patty's engagement with undisguised pleasure ; and if the pleasure was partly selfish, not unmixed with the reflection that all responsibility for their foster-child was now coming to a natural and not unhappy end, all one can say is, that there is very little good in the world at all

which is not mixed with some baser element.
As for Mr. Carlisle, he was almost as silly as
on the morning when he received Patty's
letter to tell him that she had made up her
mind to leave Canonbury Square, and had
offered herself as an assistant to Mr. and Mrs.
Whitehouse. He kissed her with the sincerest
and gentlest affection, but he could find no
words in which to express his good wishes;
and when he took her into another room to
show her the presents he had bought for her,
he could just do nothing but sob and weep,
and point to his gifts, and try to stammer out
that they were for her, as a poor token of his
love. He was a poor, blundering, good-
natured old soul—"a good man, for whom,
peradventure, one would even dare to die"—
but with no power of speech, no pretty senti-
ments and flowery words. So much the better,
thought Patty, as she saw him hurrying away
down the Square with his handkerchief to his

eyes—hurrying off to Oxford Street, as was
his way in any trouble, to see if honest work
would not dull the sharpness of its edge.   For
somehow this parting with Patty, even though
she was only going to be married, was a
trouble to him.   *Only* going to be married
indeed!

"Ah, he's very tender-hearted," said Mrs.
Carlisle, "but he's just gone down to business
to work it off a little.   You must not think he
does not approve of it, Patty, or anything of
that sort, because he's a little overcome."

And then this active, strong-minded matron
began to ask all manner of questions about the
dresses, and the breakfast, and the innumerable
trifles by which the melancholy uncertainties
that always surround a wedding are partly
disguised.

"Well, well, dear," she said, " I don't know
how they manage these things in Manchester,
but I've no doubt the Rhodeses will have

everything as it should be. I half wish we could have had the wedding in London, but of course it's all right to consider your father."

It was a thousand pities that Mrs. Carlisle could not have cooked the breakfast, and occupied all the wedding morning in talking of its merits. However, she took good care, in her bustling way, to show to Patty each and all of those presents which poor Mr. Carlisle had so inarticulately exhibited.

"We might have made them look much more," she said; "but then it's all real." Whereupon she exhibited the mark. "Of course there are many handsome things in the plated way; but what I always think is —*silver's silver*, and it will always fetch its worth, dear, however fashions may alter."

"Why, my dear Mrs. Carlisle," said Patty, "your presents are really splendid; but you must not think that I should have valued them less, whatever they had been."

"Yes, yes, my dear, that's very well, indeed; and if we could not have afforded real, we must have bought plated : but, thank God, we can. And how do you like the decanters?" she went on, putting a stopper into Patty's hand; "they are the very best cut glass we could get, as you may tell by feeling."

Of course Patty admired them very much, and thanked Mrs. Carlisle very sincerely for them, and for much more, though Mrs. Carlisle's mode of making presents was not in all respects the one she would have herself adopted. The good lady was very generous, though her generosity was not so refined and reticent as with advantage it might have been. But, after all, is not love and real silver decidedly better than love and plated goods? and is a thing less pretty or less worthy of admiration because you are giving it away to somebody else? Mrs. Carlisle was not really glorifying herself while she was making the most of the presents that she had bought for Patty; she was only trying to make them yield the full amount of satisfaction which they were capable of yielding; and Patty really was pleased with the gifts, and pleased even more with the givers. And when she left the house in Canonbury Square, it was almost with a feeling of dread that she reflected how immeasurably her condition would be altered before she crossed that threshold again.

At Oak Villa, on her last evening, there was a very different scene. There also were presents and kind wishes, and all the terrible grief and pain of separation which everybody has some time or other to go through. But Oak Villa had been for Patty almost the beginning of real life; not, indeed, that she went there without experience, but her experience before had been all of the passive, receptive sort; whereas at Oak Villa she had begun to work.

Moreover, it was the sort of work that follows people, work upon the hearts and characters of human beings, living men and women. "A thing of beauty is a joy for ever!" and there is doubtless a sort of sympathy between the artist and his work, which is a far nobler and completer reward than the loud applause of those admirers, the great majority of whom must be very incompetent judges. In the statue or painting, the artist may often read the record of his own inmost life; months, or even years of his profoundest thought and deepest emotion. He will remember, as he gazes upon his work, what visions were granted him of ideal and eternal beauty, that never in this world can find full and perfect expression. He will remember lofty aspirations, and the purifying power of perfect beauty, which made him a true man. And yet, how little can it be said, that there is any *perfect* sympathy between the artist and even the noblest work of art. What does the picture care for the painter, or the statue for the sculptor? The whole beauty of his work is that which the artist has himself given to it; and there is no new beauty gained to make his spirit richer. Nay, does not the canvas and the marble limit and spoil that grand ideal which the man's spirit had beheld and tried to copy? But when Patty was working for those poor un-happy, erring sisters who were brought to the peaceful home of Oak Villa, she could see in them far more than she ever gave. Their own life was renewed. Their love responded to hers. As she taught them, they seemed rather to remember than to learn; and out of their gratitude and recovered womanhood they gave even more than they had received.

Far into the last night she was passing from room to room, strengthening each inmate with words of love and trust; with the genuine love of a sister. Hearts that no cruellest punishment could have softened, melted in the divine fire of her charity. And when at last she retired to her own chamber, worn out with fatigue and emotion, she knelt down to thank God that she had not lived utterly in vain ; and to pray that if ever her own hour of need should come, some loving lips might with equal sincerity speak God's message to *her* weary heart. She was full of hope ; but her last night at Oak Villa seemed to reproach her. Was she not going away to ease and selfish rest, just as if all the dreadful problems of human sin and misery had been solved for ever ?

The next morning she was up early ; she wanted to get to Manchester by the fast train, and to have some brief respite from the pain and excitement of leave-taking, before the wedding-day. But there was one friend, not unremembered or unloved, to whom she had not yet ventured to say the inevitable adieu.

Should she see him at all? And yet would it not seem utterly unaccountable to leave London without the "good-bye," which each of them could say to the other so sincerely? And what meant the strange tumult in her heart, as she thought of Mr. Leighton? Were not all those old hopes dead and buried— buried in the grave of her new love? Why not go and see him and say "good-bye?" Why not, indeed! She could no more have left London without *that*, than she could have unlived the last few years of her life. So she stopped the cab at the doctor's door and went in. He was at home.

"I quite expected you this morning, Miss Wilson," he said.

"Well, Mr. Leighton, I could not leave London without bidding you good-bye— though I'm only going to be married, and I hope often to see my old friends again."

Poor Leighton! he was as pale as death; fighting with all manner of mad impulses.

"Why, indeed, should you leave us, Miss Patty, without good-bye," he said; "of course you are only going to be married, but marriage brings many cares and duties, which render the intercourse of friends rare and difficult."

"I shouldn't like to think, Mr. Leighton, that one love can kill another."

"No, no, Miss Wilson, but there are many kinds of death. Perhaps a lonely, lingering life is the worst death of all."

There was a pause. It seemed as if he had lost all command of his voice. At last he said—

"How did the girls bear your leaving them, Miss Patty?"

Patty could bear it no longer. She fairly broke down, and wept passionately.

"Oh spare me, Mr. Leighton," she said.

"That is my one trouble. Is it right to leave them ? As they spoke to me last night, I felt the most selfish, wretched creature in the world. And what can I do at Clayton's Hall but enjoy myself—while there is so much misery unrelieved ? "

" God grant that you may have nothing but joy for evermore. But if it should be otherwise—which God forbid !—if ever you are disappointed, lonely, miserable, will you remember me—that I am always your friend ? I will come at your call from the world's end. I shall hear your voice, your faintest whisper, wherever I may be, and I will be with you as swift as thought——"

He seemed scarcely to know what he was saying, borne along in the great rush of his feeling.

"No, no, forgive me, Miss Patty," he said ; " these are ill-omened words. Good-bye. May you be so utterly happy that you may never need to consider what friends you have that you may reckon upon to the uttermost."

She was gone. He had seen the last he could see; and still he stood at the window, as if he were rooted to the spot. Slowly, at last, he turned away. "My patients must do as best they can to-day," he said; and then he scorned his cowardice, fought his battle out, and won once more.

"The best comforter is duty."

Yes, truly; there could be no solace in idleness; but while he went from house to house, trying to forget his own grief in ministering to the wants of others, he could no way escape that heavy burden that was weighing down his heart. It was not only that he had lost Patty, but he had no confidence whatever in Forester. Perhaps jealousy made him quick-eyed, for every fault or weakness of his rival; but he believed him to be utterly unprincipled. He believed that he was lazily unprincipled now, and might remain so until he had stung some victim of his cold-hearted recklessness into fierce retaliation ; and then he too would fight with the unprincipled ferocity of an enraged beast of prey. And now, whatever he might be or become, Patty was going down to Manchester to take him "for better for worse—until death should them part." And he could do nothing for her—not even warn ; only in a half frantic way assure her of his help if she should ever come to need it.

And now the very day had come, and the hour ; and Patty Wilson and Edwin Marie Forester stood side by side in Cheetham Hill Church, that they might be made man and wife together. How short is the time, how few are the irrevocable words which bring such hopeless misery, where they do not bring pure and holy joy. One poor quarter of an hour, and Patty Forester's very

life was either won or thrown away beyond
recovery.

But there is scarcely time for a bride to fear
on her wedding morning. Forester was somewhat graver than usual, but Patty was well
pleased to have it so ; and he was very gentle
and affectionate, almost as tender as if he were
pitying the fair young girl, who was so confiding and good.   They went away, as had
been arranged, to the Lakes ; though Forester
never stayed more than a day at one place.

"You know, my darling," he said,—"you
can't think how delightful it is to have you
with me, and know that no one can ever take
you away—but that is not what I was going
to say."   No, it was only a little parenthetic
burst of affection ;—"but what I *was* going to
say is, that it's all very well for an artist to
sit on a cold stone on a hill-side, and spend a
whole morning in looking on another cold
stone on the other side of the valley—but we

are not artists, we are not going to paint the Lakes, nor write an interesting narrative of a honeymoon. So we just stand here, for instance, and open our eyes wide and look about us, and we see a lake and blue sky, and a hill, and green trees, and we rapidly observe the various combinations of all these different elements, and we go on our way rejoicing to something else. Besides," he said, turning round and looking into her face, " I've nothing to do, but turn my head round, when I have you at my side, and then I can see the very sight in all the world that I like best ; always the same and always different."

And then he walked on of course ; and what would have been the use of her saying that there was a good deal that she wanted to see more of. She was hardly prepared in the first week of her married life to face the absurdity of being an artist. So they went on from place to place taking a rapid glance at everything.

Forester's way of making an excursion was this. He first obtained a Bradshaw's Railway Guide; or rather, he first determined where he should go, and then he provided himself with a Railway Guide. He ascertained which would be the fastest and most luxurious train to travel by, and then the best hotel to stop at. When he arrived at the place that he had determined to honour with a visit, he of course went at once to the hotel that he had determined to stop at. He immediately ordered dinner—four or five courses, and plenty of wine; for what's the use of staying at an hotel if you do not live sumptuously? Dinner and dessert would naturally occupy the best part of the day of arrival; then in the evening he would stroll out at his leisure to ascertain what there was worth seeing in the neighbourhood; then he would order a carriage, or guide, or whatever might be necessary, and then about the middle of the next morning he would go and see it.

At dinner, after having seen what was to be seen, he would once more consult his Bradshaw, and would set off the next morning by the fastest train to the next place he had determined to visit. In this manner he could make the tour of several counties in a fortnight; and know much more about them too, than many people would have supposed possible.

"Yes," he would say, for instance, " the Peak—I have been to the Peak ; no railway at that time, nor anything comfortable ; a miserable tumble-down old coach ; heaps of nasty tiresome hills, that they make you get out of the coach to walk up, just as if you hadn't paid the coach-fare for the very purpose of being carried up. The last time I went up the Peak there was a disgusting cockatoo in the inside of the coach, belonging to a charming old lady, the clergyman's wife apparently. The animal was continually hopping down from its perch, and biting the knees of everybody who didn't give it biscuit. Of course the clergyman's wife rebuked the cockatoo for such ill-regulated behaviour; but what comfort is it, when you've had a piece bitten out of your knee, to have the cockatoo reproved? But after all," he would say, "I think the Peak is a very won-derful piece of scenery—wonderful place for artists; no end of cold stones to sit on, and draw fogs in the valley."

It must be very obvious that Mr. Edwin Forester was destitute of what is called an eye for nature; but when he had plenty of money, his own or anybody else's, as the case might be, and nothing on his mind, he was not by any means an insufferable companion. In his little wedding-tour, though Patty may have wanted to see more, she was at least enjoying her first visit to the Lakes. Everything was provided for her with an almost princely mag-nificence; for everybody knows the best people in the world to spend money are those who have no money to spend. When you are really spending your own money, the fear of extravagance and ultimate penury is ever before your eyes; but when you positively have nothing, and can only spend other people's money, you can't possibly be poorer than you are, and you may just as well be comfortable as not. At the same time, Patty was not sorry that the honeymoon was to be short. She longed to see Leigh once more, and she longed above all to settle in her own house, and face the life that was before her. She had no misgivings—at least she thought not, hoped not, tried to believe not. And yet Forester, in this first fortnight of their married life, was very different from the earnest, lonely man who had pleaded so hard for love, and help, and fellowship in the Regent's Park. He was very amusing; but he seemed to find his fun in surrounding great and holy things with ridiculous circumstances and degrading associations.   He was very kind and affectionate; but somehow Patty seemed to feel that he cared most for that which had least to do with her truest womanliness and deepest nature.

However, short or long, all trips come to an end at last; and Patty found herself one glorious autumn evening at Clayton's Hall, almost on the very spot where Edwin Marie was born, and where Marie, his mother, desolate and broken-hearted, had died.

END OF VOL. I.

www.ingramcontent.com/pod-product-compliance
Lightning Source LLC
Chambersburg PA
CBHW020854020726
47497CB00005B/1400